FLOAT UP,
SING DOWN

ALSO BY LAIRD HUNT

This Wide Terraqueous World

Zorrie

In the House of the Dark Woods

The Evening Road

Neverhome

Kind One

Ray of the Star

The Exquisite

Indiana, Indiana

The Impossibly

FLOAT UP,
SING DOWN

LAIRD HUNT

Stories

riverrun

First published in the United States in 2024 by Bloomsbury Publishing Inc.
This edition published in Great Britain in 2024 by

riverrun

An imprint of

Quercus Editions Limited
Carmelite House
50 Victoria Embankment
London EC4Y 0DZ

An Hachette UK company

A CIP catalogue record for this book is available
from the British Library.

Hardback ISBN 978 1 52943 450 7
Trade Paperback ISBN 978 1 52943 451 4
Ebook ISBN 978 1 52943 452 1

10 9 8 7 6 5 4 3 2 1

Typeset by Jouve (UK), Milton Keynes

Printed and bound in Great Britain by Clays Ltd, Elcograf S.p.A.

Papers used by Riverrun are from well-managed forests and other responsible sources.

For Linda and Chris with gratitude and love

There is nothing too small, but my tenderness paints it large on a background of gold

—RAINER MARIA RILKE

CONTENTS

Float Up, Sing Down

Candy

C andy Wilson had forgotten to buy the paprika. She had thought about it more than once that morning in town as she pushed her cart down shiny aisle after shiny aisle at the Marsh. Now it was clear to her that this thinking—this seeing of her hand scooping up the little red and white paprika tin, the way it actually scooped up eggs and orange Jell-O and pineapple and carrots and real butter and a fresh jar of Hellmann's and every single other thing on her list—had taken the place of getting it done. Meaning she had a problem. Club was set to start in just a few hours. Some of the members liked her pigs in a blanket, some her caramel corn, and Alma Dunn and Lois Burton always took seconds and sometimes even thirds of her sunshine salad, but to a rosy-red carapace every member of the Bright Creek Girls Gaming Club loved her deviled eggs. Paprika was the recipe's sine qua non, and Candy, whose turn it was, couldn't host the monthly meeting without it.

She had the eggs ready to roll. They were boiled and peeled and halved and scooped and laid out cool and white on Saran Wrap–covered trays. The vinegar was measured, and both the mustard and the Hellmann's needed only to be opened and dolloped out. Candy loved to dollop. It was one of those small things that made the big things better. First there was the weight of the whipped cream or the mashed potatoes or the cookie batter or the mayonnaise or, in the case of deviled eggs, the creamy yellow mixture the mayonnaise had brought into being. Then there was the turning of the spoon and the quick downward motion that you stopped almost at the same time you started it. So satisfying. It made Candy grin. It pleased her soul. And it didn't hurt that you sometimes had to help whatever it was you were dolloping to find its way off the spoon. For then the helping finger could be licked.

In the meantime she was nonplussed. Town was twelve miles each way. She liked driving and often made up reasons to jump in the car and go off plenty farther than Frankfort, but the clock wasn't on her side. She picked up the phone and called Alma, and Alma said try Laetitia, and Laetitia said try Zorrie, and she did but Zorrie didn't answer her phone. This was not surprising. Zorrie was still always out of doors. She was out of doors as much as many of them were indoors. Candy wondered if she ought to drive over. Probably Zorrie was out in her garden or mowing. She did a lot more of that these days than she had ever used to. Even if she didn't have any paprika they could visit for a minute. A minute couldn't hurt. Zorrie wouldn't care one bit that the paprika was for deviled eggs for a meeting of a club she was not, by choice, a member of. Candy got her keys and purse.

It was mid-July. But not too hot. A storm the night before had cooled things down. Candy drove with her arm out the window of her Buick, and if her shoulder hadn't hurt, she would have turned her hand into a hawk and let it rise and drop. Just about everyone who still earned a living on a tractor was out doing something. The sky was blue. Zorrie Underwood's acres shone bright and green and her lawn looked better than respectable. There was a garden of note peeping out from behind the barn. Candy's own garden had for years been a pitiful thing. She called it her abomination. She liked to tell people about how badly it was coming. She used the word *abomination* as often as she could. As she climbed out of the car, she saw something move and thought Zorrie's old dog, Oats, was about to come tearing around the house to holler at her, but it was just a cat. Oats of course was long gone. Candy knocked on the door but there was no answer. She sat a while on Zorrie's back steps. She could see the green roof of the Summers' house through the trees. The idea of asking old Noah Summers if he had any paprika made her chuckle. "Still, I am more nonplussed now than I was a while ago," she said to a sugary gray catbird that was pecking around near Zorrie's pillowy hydrangeas. She pulled a sticky note out of her purse, scribbled on it that she had come by to borrow paprika, stuck it on Zorrie's screen door, got back in her car, and headed for town.

Nonplussed had been a word favored by Candy's great friend Irma Ray. Irma had known all the words. For a stretch she had taught French over at the high school, where for many years Candy had served as a substitute teacher in Home Ec. Unlike some of the others who had liked to make weapons out of strings of letters just so they could smack you upside the head with them, Irma had always deployed her vocabulary for the good. Too many to count were the times Irma had sat in Candy's kitchen and watched Candy at her dolloping and, just by the way she said something, helped Candy to think more clearly about whatever issue had vultured down on her day. After Irma had stopped teaching and started tutoring out of her house, she and Candy had become even closer. Irma's skill with words had not made her popular with the girls in the club, and she had attended only once as Candy's special guest. Still, she was the one who had suggested Candy always splurge on Hellmann's for her deviled eggs and that she use butter instead of Crisco for her cozy little pigs. Who said you couldn't teach an old Home Ec teacher new tricks? Following Irma's advice had made all the difference. Club at Candy's house was considered something you could not miss. It was the apex of the yearly club calendar. Irma would have had paprika on hand. Her headstone had been standing over at Bright Creek's Bakerworth cemetery for a year now.

The Marsh was busier than Candy liked when she had an errand to execute, and of course, since she was in a hurry, she saw about one hundred people she knew. She had been a popular substitute teacher and for a while a fixture at Elks events across the county with her took-off husband, Frank. She might well have been retired from teaching, but she still couldn't come into town without getting struck up by familiar faces. Today, it was like bugs on a windshield, the big splattery kind. First there was a family of Newtons and then another of Thompsons. The Thompsons had a new baby in their number, so Candy couldn't just wave and keep on. The baby was asleep, so the visiting was conducted at a whisper, lest the little banshee awake. There was something to say about someone's aunt's surgery. Also, the mother of the baby wanted to show that she still had her hospital bracelet on. She said she was going to wear it until little Deirdre's first tooth came in. Ordinarily it was Candy who kept the bellows blowing on a conversation, but the clock was ticking so she made her excuses, bent and cooed over baby Deirdre, and then pressed on. Earl Crick, who had been in the Elks with Frank, slowed her up in Floral long enough for her to decide to put a bouquet of yellow roses in her basket. Earl's wife, Selah, had made a presentation at church about keeping a spiritual diary a few weeks before. Thinking about keeping a spiritual diary made Candy laugh. What would be the point of it? What would she write? She hadn't ever seen anyone walking on water. She hadn't seen any burning bush. What she could see, through the window, was her cousin's great-nephew, Tod Henry, chasing carts in the parking lot. At some point he'd grown handsome. Or almost. It sometimes happened. She wondered if he'd developed good manners to go with the cheekbones and shoulders. The little white-topped red tin of Durkee paprika looked pretty next to the roses. Beryl Reedy was at the register, and because it was clear that she was working up something to say about the flowers to do with one of her soap operas that was way more complicated than it had to be and would take a while to get said, Candy cut her off. "Club day. I forgot the paprika. We got bingo going this month."

Bingo was actually Razzle Dazzle, and it was everyone's favorite. They all got dressed up like they made their living in a gambling hall and put on visors, and some of them, Candy included, even wore pink or purple eyeglasses. Each girl had her own marbles and made a fuss about them. Lois had the nicest ones. She'd brought them back from a trip to see her niece who ran a cake shop down in Louisville. The club's newest member,

Gladys Bacon, had marbles filled with glitter. The marbles were just cheap glass but the glitter was all different colors. She kept them in a red and yellow silk bag they'd given out at the Panda House buffet one Christmas. You couldn't put up less than a quarter. In all their other games the minimum was a penny. They used a score chart that made it easier to win, but you still had to work at it. Cheating was tolerated though not openly encouraged. Some of the girls took it more seriously than was strictly necessary. That happened sometimes when they played their euchre tournaments too. Candy was a hand-straight-up-in-the-air offender when it came to cards. Win or lose, she always slapped her play down too hard. Razzle Dazzle mostly just made her laugh. She especially liked the sound of the marbles as they hit the board and rolled around crazy until they found their holes.

At the one club meeting Irma Ray had come to, Razzle Dazzle had been on the menu. Candy had put a spare visor on Irma's head and the two of them had played Candy's marbles. Afterward, as she had helped clean up, Irma had voiced her admiration both for the game's "bizarreries" and for the club members' bawdy-house costumes. Candy, maybe too eager to broach the subject of possible membership for Irma, had repeated Irma's observations at the start of the next meeting. Irma had said she thought the debauched court of King Louis the Fourteenth at Versailles would have liked Razzle Dazzle, and Candy, though she immediately thought better of it afterward, especially of including the word *debauched*, reported this too. The reaction of the girls was not what Candy had been hoping for. It was clear that there had been prior discussion among them. Alma summed it up nice and neat by saying maybe there ought to be a limit on special guests coming to club. That maybe once was plenty.

Others nodded. Some looked away. There was a good deal of slurping and loud chewing. Candy shut the subject down with a sharp, "Well she doesn't want to come back anyway."

Which hadn't been anything but the truth. Even if she had gotten the girls to go along with it, Candy had been sure that Irma—whose tastes in entertainment ran in different directions—would not have accepted. But Candy had wanted to be able to put it to her. Irma would have appreciated that. Candy had pulled out of the Marsh with the intention of getting home as quickly as possible to dollop and mix, then dollop again and sprinkle, but almost as if they had started making their own decisions while she got grumpy, Candy found her foot pumping the brakes and then her hands turning the steering wheel so that she could cut over off 28 to the Kelly Road. By itself, this wouldn't have been much of a detour, except that when she had slid east along its smooth blacktop past the Red Barn Theater, where she and Irma had taken in many a show, she turned right instead of left onto 421 and rolled south to Bright Creek and then, after honking at Turner Davis, who was working a hoe in his front flower bed on North Main, west out to the Bakerworth cemetery so that, on this anniversary of Irma's quiet funeral—which had been attended only by Candy, Zorrie, Hank Dunn, Toby Slocum, and two or three at the most others—she could pay a quick tribute.

One of the yellow roses came out of the car with her. When she was halfway across the grass, she stopped, turned, went back to the car, and fetched up the rest of them too. Irma had always been partial to cut flowers, and you about hadn't been able to step into her house without smelling lilies, peonies, or roses. Yellow in any shade had without question been her favorite color. Irma hadn't lived particularly close to the Bakerworth cemetery and might more logically have chosen Beech Hill, but she had always favored Bakerworth. Said she liked the way the countryside rolled out clear in all directions. Said a cemetery ought to have some view. Candy could remember the day when Irma had announced the purchase of her plot. It hadn't been very long before they had lowered her box into it. She'd always had money. Single woman with a job. Her tutoring work wasn't much, but she still had money in the bank and had owned her house outright. It was why she had been able to go off on trips. Candy hadn't gone with her on any of those. They never even ventured outside the county together. Candy had postcards from Miami, New Orleans, and San Francisco. Though Irma had been to Paris and Rome in her youth, the farthest she got during the years Candy knew her was up in Canada. She brought Candy back a stuffed grizzly bear from that trip. It had a ribbon around its neck that read "Dawson City." Candy kept it on a shelf in her bedroom.

The cemetery had a healthy look. The daylilies were up in force, and there were sweat bees hanging easy in the air. The grass had been mowed recently enough that it tickled her nose, and there were bright green trimmings even up on the top of Irma's headstone. Candy swept them off with the back of her hand. The smooth, black stone was warm. Letting her hand lie there a minute, she closed her eyes and hummed a little. It was something she did when she visited Irma's grave. She did it instead of talking or praying. Well, she sometimes prayed a little too: for Irma's easy passage, her safe departure, the heap of fresh adventures she had ahead of her now. You had to think God would be helping out. Candy had gone so far as to ask the reverend one Sunday after church if he thought God showered his favor on people who were different. "Different how?" the reverend had asked. Different how indeed? Irma had had the Latin phrase "Astra Inclinant Sed Non Obligant" engraved on her stone.

Candy put the radio on for the drive home. It was a pop station out of Lafayette. Generally she liked whatever was on. Unlike Lois and Alma who turned up their noses, she thought what got played these days was better than most of the old chestnuts. She had never been able to stand Elvis Presley even though plenty of them still got moony-faced whenever "Hound Dog" or "Love Me Tender" came on. She had left the flowers standing against Irma's grave. She knew they would fall over the first time the wind cleared its throat, but for now they were standing tall and would keep standing for a little while and that was about all you could hope for. Next time she would bring a vase. She kept meaning to. Irma deserved that. She deserved a hundred vases. Candy hoped that's just what she had, a hundred flower-filled vases, wherever she was. Somehow or other, before Candy left, her hand had again followed its own orders and reached into her purse and pulled out the tin of paprika to set atop the warm black stone. She thought she would just leave it there a minute, but it looked so nice with the yellow of the roses and the black of the stone and the green of the fresh-cut grass that after she hummed some more she walked away without taking it with her. She would put pepper on the eggs. Maybe add some cayenne. Let the girls Razzle Dazzle that down. What was wrong with being different? It was exactly what Frank had called her plenty of times and she'd done all right. He called her that the night they had fought for the last time and she told him that if he slapped her just once more she would put an axe between his eyes as he slept. She grabbed up the Bible and took an oath about it. Frank slapped her exactly once more and then got in his car and never came back.

Candy looked right, then left, when she got to Bright Creek. If she turned right, she could roll straight to Indianapolis. She had always thought one day she would drive down there. See for herself who it was Irma had kept running down to visit. They never once talked about it, but Candy knew the address. She had carried Irma's mail up to the house from the box at the road more than once on her visits. The envelopes were turquoise. Irma had burned all the letters before taking her leave and a breeze must have come up because there were bits of burnt turquoise caught in Irma's hollyhocks and dahlias. Candy plucked one of these from a crimson bloom and kept it for good luck. Turner, who had been seeing to his zinnias, was no longer in his yard. Candy liked a nice zinnia but Irma had not. She said they had funny connotations for her. The girls would be arriving in an hour. Candy was cutting it close. They would all be on time. It was not the kind of club where anyone ever arrived late.

Irma had rarely been on time. In fact, she had been late even the day she pulled up in her nifty yellow Chevy Nova coupe as a special guest to play Razzle Dazzle and eat refreshments with the club. Candy had liked this about her. Most people said she was standoffish and not much fun, but she hadn't been either of those things, not when you got to know her. When you got to know her, you could never tell what she would say or do. Things had not been easy for Irma at the high school. The vice principal had taken her aside any number of times. It was the principal, not the vice principal, though, who asked Irma to step into his office not long after the rumors started to run. And it was the principal, after someone had seen Irma and her coupe down in Indianapolis, who told her she had better gather up her things.

Candy had gone straight over to see Irma when she heard. There was a Billie Holiday record on the player, and Irma was sitting close to the speaker, swirling a glass of wine. "Got an idea," she told Candy. The back seat of the Nova was covered with rolls of toilet paper. It was game night in basketball season, so everyone was over watching the orange ball go bouncing up and down the court at the high school. The principal had persimmons, crab apples, and pear trees that lent themselves especially well to the exercise. Candy wasn't much of a hand at throwing, but Irma could really heave. They made the vice principal's ranch house, garage, and gazebo their primary targets at the next stop. Irma dedicated each roll to a different insult she'd received from him: short skirt; see-through blouse; sour expression; sick, sick, sick ideas. When they got back to Irma's, Candy, who never drank, allowed herself a splash of wine. Irma, meanwhile, polished off the bottle. And after a few glasses her mood shifted. She said some things in French that didn't sound good. When she switched back to English, she told Candy that the principal had probably been right to fire her. She had dressed improperly, she had spoken inappropriately, she had taught racy novels, and she had—oh yes she had—misbehaved. Candy shushed her, made her something to eat that she wouldn't touch and then put her to bed. As Candy was leaving, Irma said in a small voice that the person she went down once each month to see in Indianapolis wasn't even nice to her, and she didn't know why she hadn't been able to quit going there. Candy said what Irma did was her own business and she didn't have to explain anything. Irma responded that she had often wished it was

Candy, not that unkind person, who lived in the little blue house behind the high bushes at the end of the street in Indianapolis.

Candy had never lived anywhere in her adult life but in the house she had inherited from her parents. It was a nice place. Even Frank had always said so. He had never minded living there, especially since there hadn't been any rent or mortgage to pay. As she pulled into the driveway, she looked upon the neat lines and tidy white paint and clean windows and sturdy roof and respectable flower beds. It was true that her lawn needed the mowing that she now wouldn't have time to give it and of course there was the abomination out back, but you couldn't get everything done. Everything wasn't possible. Everything wasn't even anything she had ever wanted. For a long time, she'd raised chickens but they had finally worn her out, so she had let her band of merry seed snackers go. Sometimes she missed the birds themselves but not the waking up early to tend them. Still, they had kept her somewhat in shape. Irma had often said she, too, ought to have chickens, that she appreciated how having them made a person stir around. There had been the smell though. Candy and Irma had laughed about it, but on a hot day it had filled the house. Candy was glad that the girls arriving soon wouldn't have to contend with that.

The time for raising chickens had passed, but Candy knew she was going to have to do something to get herself into shape. Her back and left shoulder hurt worse than usual and she was short on breath from her errand, and the push to get ready for the meeting kept making her want to sit down. She had a doctor who said every time she went in to get her blood pressure checked that she needed to lose twenty pounds. It was always twenty even when she had gained some. If she had had time, she would have drawn a bath and then taken a quick nap. But she did not have time. And now she felt foolish for leaving the paprika behind. Like anyone else she could be a little sharp sometimes, but she did not like to think of herself as spiteful. She would just put a little salt on the eggs. There wasn't any call for cayenne pepper. It wasn't like any of the girls had ever been flat-out mean about Irma Ray. Sometimes some of them had even asked after her. When they had all seen one another at the Red Barn or at the cinema in Frankfort or at the Jim Dandy or Ponderosa, it had always been cordial. Everyone had particular friends. Everyone ran around. After word of Irma's death got out, a few of them—though none of them had attended the funeral—had called Candy up to express their condolences. Lois had said how sorry she was that Irma had felt badly enough that she needed to do it.

Candy dolloped and mixed, then scooped and dolloped. Thinking about those twenty pounds and all she was going to allow herself in the coming hours, she waited to lick her finger until every last egg had been filled. How many devils would she eat? She'd get her share. She was about to start sprinkling the salt when she heard a knock on the front screen. She took a bet with herself that it was Myrtle Kelly. Myrtle was famous for her loud laugh and for always wanting to be the first person at the parade. Or it might be Gladys. Gladys liked to arrive early just in case she needed to leave early, which she almost always did. Probably it was both of them, since they often rode together. "It's open!" Candy hollered. When neither Myrtle nor Gladys nor anyone else came in though, she wiped her hands, took off her apron, and, still certain it was someone with a cup and marbles in her hand, picked up her visor and pulled her little purple sunglasses on. But when she tugged open the door, she saw

Zorrie Underwood, cast in purple, pulling away in her truck. On
Candy's front steps sat a tin of paprika with a note under it that
read, "Had it for a while but there ought to be enough dynamite left in here to get the job done."

Zorrie, Zorrie, Zorrie. Always there. Never any fuss. Didn't
matter if you wanted to borrow milk or paprika or had some
acres you needed plowed. Candy would save her an egg. Maybe
she would save out two. That way Zorrie could give one of them
to Noah Summers. Zorrie was in love with Noah. Everyone
knew it. Life was funny like that. All those little secrets that
weren't secrets at all. Moving quickly but carefully, Candy
opened the tin and tapped her way down the rows. She didn't
like to scatter the paprika too freely. She wasn't throwing rice
at a wedding or tossing confetti around. There was a way to do
it even when you only had about a minute before people started
banging on your door. That was something she had talked about
in her classes. She could have been the regular teacher. Everyone
always said so. The same vice principal who had taken Irma
aside had even mentioned it, but then he asked Candy out and
she turned him down and that was the end of that. She and
Irma laughed about it later. It even came up one of the last
times they saw each other. It was the evening that Irma put a
record on and, when a slow song started to play, held out a
hand and asked Candy if, well, she would care to dance. Candy
had said yes, yes by God she would care to dance, and they had
gone turning close and slow around the room. At one point
during that dance Irma leaned in and whispered what she
referred to as an additional request, and after they took another
turn across the soft carpet Candy again said yes. She said yes, yes
of course, and then they both laughed about it, and the evening
carried on and they saw each other a couple more times, and

then, according to the inquest, Irma hanged herself in the shed. Hank Dunn was the one to find her. Nobody thought that was strange. They'd been friendly for a long time. Candy worked with Hank to make sure Irma's wishes were respected: simple funeral, no viewing, coffin closed.

Candy finished tapping out the paprika and licked her finger. She'd got the mixture right. Warm and smoky. Almost sweet. She took two deviled eggs off the tray, wrapped them in plastic, and put them in the fridge. Standing there with the cool pouring out and the two eggs tinted purple, Candy smiled, smiled about her great friend Irma Ray, off on her next journey, though after a minute she found herself wishing so hard her head began to hurt that she still had reason to set aside a third. That evening, when the girls finally grew tired of marbles and quarters and cheating, and Laetitia suggested, without in any real way meaning it, that they put on some music and cut a rug, Candy almost leaped out of her seat to switch on the radio. The song that was playing pleased no one. Not even Candy. Still, after everyone had gone home, and she had taken off her visor and glasses and cleared away everything she had the strength to, and was thinking about the bath she'd wanted earlier, and about the sweet, soft mercies of her bed, she tried the radio again.

She got it on just in time to hear the final few notes of what must have been a very pretty song. And then there was a silence. And then the fine, deep voice of an announcer rumbled in like last night's storm. The voice reminded Candy a little of her father's. Her father had liked to carry her on his shoulders. He had liked to swing her around. He would swing Candy around and around, and when he let her go, she would lie there laughing on the grass. The world spun and Candy couldn't stop laughing. Sometimes when she visited Irma's grave, when she was done humming, she laughed. She had done it again today. As she went back to the car. She had turned around then and winked at the stone, at the flowers, at the bright little paprika can and the blue of the sky beyond. According to Laetitia, Candy had outdone herself with the deviled eggs, they were the best ever "The best ever," Candy said to the empty room. She switched off the radio. She went upstairs. "Now how about that?" her father had always said.

Turner

Turner Davis needed to get his zinnias in. Well, first he needed to get his zinnias. They were waiting for him over at Emerald Sylvester's Garden Emporium east of Tipton. Emerald Sylvester always had the best zinnias in the brightest colors, and they had been ready to be fetched for going on two weeks. Thing of it was, Turner's truck was in the shop. Usually it was about the carburetor, and Cubby Rogers had him back in business before he could blink. But here he still truckless was. Turner's wife, Jodi, said there wasn't any hurry, that Cubby had had things on his mind, the poor man, and Turner ought to just be patient. He could work on the fence, which had taken another beating in last night's weather, or help her some more in the garden. Turner didn't have what he needed to fix the fence, and he had no interest in doing any more than he already did in Jodi's garden. Jodi had that under control anyway. She was getting compliments. There had been an abundance already this year of radishes, green beans, and zucchini, practically every single one of which he had harvested and washed.

The beds were Turner's department. He had cleared out everything and dug and amended and turned and raked and now it was just the rich black dirt ready for its oranges and reds and lavenders and yellows and purples and greens. Turner had spent so much time thinking about it that he'd started seeing zinnias in his dreams. Generally, the dreams he remembered in the morning were pleasant things, but these ones to do with the zinnias sitting in their pots over at Emerald Sylvester's were not. They made him feel like he was late for summer. Like he was late for his whole life. When he had tried to explain his dreams to Jodi, she had got her someone-please-change-the-channel-or-swear-to-God-I'm-going-to-shoot-myself look, so he had stopped. He had better luck with Champ Cullen, who lived three houses and a garbage-y mulberry thicket away. Champ had a Pinto with a trailer permanently attached to it. The welded-on trailer had to do with some scheme or another that hadn't played out. Story so far of Champ's life. When Turner finished telling about his dream, Champ said, "Hell, Turner, I'll give you a ride."

Luckily, Turner had brought his billfold and didn't need to go back to the house to get it. If he had gone back to the house, he would have had to explain to Jodi that he had accepted Champ's offer of help. Any time Champ offered to help, even if it was just to hold a ladder or jump-start the truck, he asked for a loan. Champ had loans out all over town. Jodi had gotten to the point that she would physically restrain Turner if the subject of asking Champ to help out with something came up. She would wrap her arms around Turner or she would lie down on top of him and she wouldn't let up until the folly had passed.

Jodi was strong. Turner wasn't any kind of a weakling, but he had a heart that wouldn't behave. It was his heart that had made him put away his broom and mop and bucket and after thirty-five years quit being a custodian over at the high school. He had been planning on ruling the hallways for at least another ten. He had liked his work. It was honest, easy but not too easy and most days almost interesting. It bothered him that his heart, which he had always been able to count on, had found a way to be so faithless to him.

Anyway, truth was Turner had brought his billfold along, hoping Champ would offer to help. He had told Jodi he was heading out for smokes, which was a joke between them, since even if he had chewed tobacco for a while, he had never once in his life had a lit cigarette in his mouth. Heading out for smokes just meant he was going for a walk. Walking was a joy in Turner's life. When he walked through Bright Creek, everyone waved. He and Jodi were well-liked. He had had his job, and Jodi had kept books and answered phones first at the grain elevator and then over at Ransom's until about yesterday. She still went in some weekends to help out. Neither one of them was that old. Jodi was probably the reason everyone was as friendly as they were. Everyone liked Jodi. Turner liked her plenty too. Or maybe admired her plenty was more like it. He frequently said that if he hadn't partnered up with Jodi, only half the people would have raised their hand when he walked by. If she was present, Jodi would usually counter with three quarters. They had a lot of jokes between them. Sometimes it seemed like too many jokes. Turner couldn't remember the last time even just a peck on the cheek hadn't made Jodi's eyebrow raise. Still, she liked him. He didn't have any doubts about that. And she would forgive him this flowery trespass. Champ only owed them seventy-five dollars, and if another something got itself added to the tab, it wouldn't be anything like the end of the world.

Turner did his thinking on this while Champ got his rig ready for the road. The passenger side of the Pinto looked like some dumpster contents had got spilled in by mistake. Turner offered to help clear the trailer at least, but Champ waved him off. He bent and lifted and swept things aside with impressive energy for a while and then he went over to the house, opened the porch door and hollered. By and by Champ's teenage son Greg came shuffling out with a mostly empty laundry basket. As he stood holding it, Champ transferred some of the bric-a-brac he had excavated from the Pinto.

"Been meaning to do this for a while," he said.

Greg wore a green headband that looked like it had been torn from an old T-shirt. He was on the thicker side. Champ had grown himself some middle over the years, but he still had slim legs from his athlete days. Greg looked like his torso had been bolted onto a pair of those old concrete mile markers.

"Don't lock your knees," Champ told him. "He always locks his knees," he said to Turner.

Greg gave no sign that he had heard or that he was hearing anything at all, and when the basket was full, he pivoted without a word and headed back into the house. Champ fussed a while over the trailer, and then followed in after Greg, and about two minutes later came out with a gigantic plastic cup. You could see some fizz rising up over the rim. Champ was known for always driving with soda even when it was cold out. There was a space he could wedge it between the seat and the emergency break. He claimed with some regularity to have never spilled a drop.

"I've never been back ended and blown up either," Champ said with a laugh after he had wedged the cup and they had gotten started. Of course now the trailer helped to keep people off his tail. People wouldn't sexy dance a trailer the way they would when it was just the car. This was why he had had it welded on. After word had gotten out about Pintos catching fire if you smacked them a sharp one on the behind, Champ had had the distinct impression that people were making it a special point to get right up on him. He knew three other people in the county who had Pintos and all said the same. Back in high school, when he had bought the Pinto out of his earnings at the country club in Frankfort, everyone had wanted a ride. He had given so many rides he'd had to replace the tires after less than a year. Now no one, not even Greg, wanted a ride in Champ's old Pinto, which was why, Champ explained pleasantly, things had gotten so cluttered up. "Someone riding shotgun makes this just like the old days," Champ said.

Turner wasn't too sure about the "just like" part. For one thing there was some smell to the car, even cleaned out as it was, plus the windshield was badly cracked and the dashboard looked like it had been slashed with a knife. Turner could remember something about those old days when Champ's Pinto was new and he would park it at an angle so that it took up two spots in the high school parking lot. There had at the time been some undeniable shine to Champ's world and what it looked like he might get up to in it with his shiny blue Pinto. Champ had been a varsity doubles tennis player and had just missed making it to state in golf. There had been girlfriends by the bushel basket when the ride was fresh and Champ still cut a splashy athlete's figure and earned that good money as an assistant pro at the

club. Turner could remember some of those girlfriends. One of
them had resulted in Greg.

Unlike his car, Champ hadn't gone entirely to seed, even if
Jodi said that with his pink and peach knock-off Izods he was
starting to look like a diabetic flamingo. Turner had to squint
and imagine to see what she meant. Champ hadn't been like
one of those former athletes who finished school, super-glued
one of their hands to a beer cooler, and straightaway slapped on
fifty pounds. Champ still had his blue eyes and most of his blond
hair and the old white tennis shorts still fit, though there was
the stomach pushing out against those light-colored Izods to
contend with. The stomach looked uncomfortable. It was big
but didn't move at all when the Pinto hit a bump and the trailer
gave out a boom and rattle. Champ didn't drink while he drove.
Turner wondered if part of the trick was he never touched the
cup once it was wedged in and the car was moving. It was true
that full as it was none of the liquid seemed to spill out.

Emerald Sylvester's was a nice chunk of road past Tipton, but
it wasn't anything like galloping up to Fort Wayne or over to
Noblesville or Crawfordsville or something along those lines.
Not that Turner wouldn't have gone that far for Emerald's
zinnias. The rest of what she grew was handsome sure enough,
but the first time Turner had laid eyes on her zinnias, he knew
he wouldn't wear himself out any more about growing his own
up from seed. Lord, that woman knew how to set a zinnia up for
success. You put some of Emerald Sylvester's zinnias in your
beds, and it was like you'd planted fireworks in your yard. Price
was fair too. Turner wondered how she stayed in business. Last
night's storm had delivered a soaking rain and the beds were
ready. Before he had gone out for smokes, he'd picked up stray
sticks and leaves and given it all one last good scrape with the hoe.

Candy Wilson had honked at him while he was at it. Candy was a talker like Champ, who was now on to advertising a job prospect that didn't sound anything like rock solid over at Frito-Lay. The prospect was connected to a friend who had once been a rival of Champ's at school. It had not been a friendly rivalry. Turner could remember them fighting more than once in the hallways. When Turner mentioned this, Champ said they had patched it all up. Champ had had many jobs over the years. This prompted him to get into when he had worked at the county jail. It was an elaborate accounting. Candy Wilson would have talked but she would also have listened. Turner could have said how excited he was to be finally going over to fetch his zinnias. He could have talked about how he felt like his truck had betrayed him and that it had pained him to wait. Getting his zinnias in and seeing to them was the main thing he did with his summers now. One year, the *Frankfort Times* had sent a photographer over to take a picture of his beds for a story on flower gardens in the area. That had been some while ago now, but everyone still remembered it.

At the light where 28 intersected 31, Champ reached his hand down and ran a surprisingly small, thin finger around the rim of his plastic cup. Then he dipped the finger in the cola, pulled it up to his mouth, and sucked for a minute at the tip. "You can't beat RC," Champ said when he was done. He then launched into a story that involved Greg and the ninth-grade English teacher. It wasn't easy to tell if Greg was the hero of the story or if the teacher was. Turner wondered if Champ would ask him before or after they got the zinnias if he could have another loan. He wondered if the story about Greg and the teacher was part of the pitch. There was a complexity to this kind of proceeding that Turner, who had never borrowed so much as a cup of sugar, found mind-boggling. You might think it was straightforward—that of course Champ would ask when the zinnias had been loaded up and Turner had been pushed to the point of peak happiness—but when there were multiple loans at multiple amounts with insufficient but not nonexistent repayment over a considerable stretch of years, the math to it just wasn't the same. Certainly, the story about the job prospect at Frito-Lay had been groundwork. Jodi said Champ owed money to more than a dozen people. Jodi knew these kinds of things. She said Champ had tried his sneaky wiles out on her one time, but she had just shut her mouth and raised her eyebrow and looked him up and looked him down, so he had slunk away.

While Champ went on, Turner tried to guess whether Emerald would have his zinnias in the front or the back lot. If he had called ahead, she would have had them waiting out front with a couple of her helpers to get them loaded up quick, but he had not been able to call because then Jodi would have known what he was up to. Jodi had ears like an elephant, plus there was a light that lit up red on the phone inside the garden shed when the line was being used. Jodi kept the phone sitting inside the shed window where she could hear and see it both. If it was being used without it first ringing, she would have wanted to know what it was about. She might even have come straight inside to investigate. Turner didn't place many phone calls. He was liked well-enough, but he did not have many friends. Jodi had long since given up on trying to get him to work on this. As far as he was concerned, he had plenty of people he could pass the time of day with, and then there was Jodi for all the rest. Problem was, Jodi thought this "all the rest" was too much. It wore her out. Jodi had plenty of friends. She did things like bowl with them over at Kokomo or take in movies and garden shows.

They were through Tipton, and Champ was talking about Greg's mother now. Turner wasn't sure what had gotten him onto that. Champ was talking about how when things had gotten hard, she had taken to staying up all night drinking decaf. She would brew herself a pot about the time Champ was turning in and she would nurse on it all night. She would sit out on the screened-in porch and smoke Dorals until the sun came up, and when Champ would go out to ask her whether she was ever going to come to bed, she would just keep slurping away on that decaf, and if he offered a penny for her thoughts, she would smile and either not answer or say, "Secret things, Champy."

"'Champy' was what she always called me," Champ said.

"Secret things like what?" Turner asked.

"She wouldn't ever tell me."

Champ chuckled and dipped his finger in his drink again. Turner turned his head and looked out the window at the woods and fields rolling by. His own secret was that he had once been a promising ballroom dancer. He had discovered his talent when it was too late to matter, when he was already a janitor and about to get himself partnered up. It had started because he had taken to sometimes watching a little of the school dance classes when he had work in the gym. Something about the way Miss Eloise Carrington moved her arms and pointed her shoe when she was showing her awkward charges the steps gave him the idea to try taking a few turns himself. He took to it when the school emptied out. In his heavy work boots, in the half dark with the waltz records playing. Turned out this kind of movement was the easiest thing in the world. Unlike Miss Carrington's students, he had not had to force his body to follow the tune. It had simply slipped it on like a nice jacket, and this jacket fit better than anything he had ever worn. He saved up and bought some smooth-soled leather shoes like the ones the men on the record covers had. He started staying late every weeknight and coming in on some of the weekends. All he had to do was watch even just part of a lesson during the day and then he could dance it that night. He added flourishes of his own. He liked the way his arm felt when it went rising up and up through the air. He liked it better than anything. One evening he dropped the record needle earlier than usual and when the first song was over saw Miss Carrington standing at the gym door.

"My good God, Mr. Davis," she said.

They sat down together on the bleachers. Miss Carrington spoke a great deal and very quickly. She could teach him a few more things, but only just a few, for she was really a pianist by training and certainly not a dancer. There was a school she could recommend in Lafayette. An even better one not too far from where she was from in Indianapolis.

Turner couldn't quite remember why it had seemed like he needed to hang it all up after that. It hadn't been anything he wasn't supposed to be doing but somehow being seen meant to him it was done. Miss Carrington nodded and smiled when she saw him in the hallways afterward, and once or twice brought up the follow-up lessons she had spoken of, but they hadn't fixed a time and she left the school abruptly before the end of the year.

After they were married, Jodi asked him once why he owned such fancy shoes. He didn't tell her. And not because he was sure she would laugh about it. Laugh about him staying late at the high school to dance and dance, to fly across the floor with his arms wrapped snug around nothing but the night. Turner liked it when Jodi laughed at him about this or that. He had liked this from the start. He just hadn't told her.

Had kept it to himself. For himself. Had kept it in reserve. He had felt good while he was dancing on the shiny gym floor. It made him think about when he was a boy, when whole afternoons lay ahead of him, afternoons he could fill full with whatever he wanted.

Turner never learned where Miss Carrington had gone. As far as he knew, there hadn't ever been any explanation for her departure. Someone said she had moved back home. The new music teacher had neither included dance nor music appreciation in her lessons, so the record player stayed sitting on a table with rollers in a storage closet near the music room for a long time. Sometimes Turner had opened the closet and turned the light on just to look at it. He wondered what Champ's ex-wife's secrets had been. He was glad Champ didn't know.

Emerald Sylvester's was a pair of big greenhouses, a triple row of shade tarps, and several sheds full of fertilizer and mulch. Emerald had done her usual sturdy work with the begonias and geraniums, and her cosmos, marigolds, and fuchsia shone so bright you'd have to worry about your eyeballs if you looked at them too long. While Champ sat in the Pinto with his giant cup at last in hand, Turner went around back to look for Emerald. He stopped along the way to admire the cleome and to measure the snapdragons, which were already up to his waist. People who bought their plants at Emerald's joked that either she put radium in her products or she was casting spells on them.

Jodi said it was easy to make jokes like that when the person you were looking for laughs about had an accent, even as incidental a one as Emerald—who had been born Esmeralda Sylvestro in Guadalajara, Mexico—had. Turner didn't doubt it. It made sense to him that there was something between the kinds of remarks and teasing everyone fired off at everyone just about all the time and the hateful things that came slithering out of certain mouths whenever their owner had come back home from Gary or Indianapolis or had just been over to eat at the Taco Bell. Turner couldn't find Emerald but he did find her husband, Hector, who was on his knees fiddling with a soaker hose near the hydrangea pots. There was a smell of wet wood and geraniums. Turner generally didn't care how flowers smelled. Hector had a tape player going. Mexican music. Sweet voices singing in Spanish. Lots of trumpets. Some kind of a guitar. Slow and strange. It took Hector a minute to stand up. When he did and Turner said what he was after, Hector looked confused.

Turner was glad when he got back to the Pinto that Champ had wandered away. He wanted a minute before he had to explain that there wouldn't be any hauling to do, that Emerald had decided it couldn't wait any longer and had gotten in her truck and taken Turner's zinnias over to Bright Creek to surprise him. Champ would find it funny, and under other circumstances it might have amused Turner too. But Hector had told Turner about his zinnias with tears trickling down his face. He had told Turner that in addition to offering the pleasure of a surprise, Emerald had felt his zinnias were at "their glory" and could not be held any longer, that it was a matter of professional pride for her, that she felt some of her reputation was at stake. The tears had trickled the whole time Hector spoke, and when Turner got out his wallet to settle, Hector's lip had quivered a little. It had only quivered the once, but there had been no mistaking it. Turner had not wanted to insult Hector by asking him what was wrong. He hoped wherever Champ had wandered off it wasn't in Hector's direction. Champ wasn't anything like mean, but you wouldn't stand up in a court of law and call him nice either.

Turner leaned against the passenger door of the Pinto. There was a heat in the air and the honeybees were having a big time over around the marigolds. Turner loved a good old-fashioned honeybee. He had often told Jodi that if he could come back as anything he wanted that was what he would choose. Jodi said he was practically a honeybee already the way he carried on about flowers. Thinking about this made Turner smile. It made him keep smiling to think of Champ's wife sitting out on the screened-in porch with her cigarettes and her decaf and her secrets. Turner wondered if Jodi would be mad when he got back now that the flowers had been delivered. He didn't think so. She would appreciate that he and Emerald had had the same idea. It would make a good story to tell her friends when they went bowling. He wouldn't say anything about Hector crying. That wasn't anyone's business but Hector's. Which was different than a secret. Or didn't necessarily make it one. There were always these kinds of gradations. For all Turner knew, Hector would have told him the whole story if he had asked. Maybe he was desperate for someone to ask. Maybe he would have told him to come inside the office, had him sit down on either the armchair or the couch, both of which were entirely covered in plastic, and given him a cup of coffee and told him about the cousin who had died, or the serious trouble he and Esmeralda were having, or a tale of some long-lost love. Turner hoped it wasn't anything too terrible. Probably it wasn't. Some people were sensitive. Maybe Hector had been thinking about a novel he had read or a favorite television show.

Jet-black dragonflies had joined the bees over the marigolds. They would dart out over the daylilies growing along the fence, then swoop back. Turner had a good sense of what bees got up to, but he had never quite figured dragonflies out. Watching them, he had an image bubble up from one of those endless summer afternoons of his early days. He and a friend were in the friend's back yard. Dragonflies like these were working over the uncut grass there. By and by, the trine of big kittens he and his friend had been lazily playing with got interested in the dragonflies. As one, they fanned out into the grass and began jumping up into the air. He and his friend were surprised by how high they could already jump. They would fly up out of the tall grasses, then vanish back into them. Over and over they leapt. Finally Turner and his friend grew bored of all the leaping without any catching and went off to do something else. What had the dragonflies been doing then and what were they doing now? Maybe he would ask Jodi. Jodi didn't have all the answers, but she always had an opinion and most of the time that was just as good.

Turner decided that instead of it being a loan he would pay Champ for helping him. That was the way to do it. He had two twenties left in his wallet, and when Champ got back from whatever it was he was doing he would just hand him one. Turner wondered where Jodi would have Emerald set the zinnias. Probably next to where the hose ran along the side of the house. Turner could see himself reaching down for a set of pots, could feel his hand closing around the trowel, could feel it slicing into the good, rich dirt.

A generator he hadn't even realized had been running stopped, and Turner heard Hector's music again. It was a different song now, a little faster than the previous one but still not fast. Turner tilted his head to hear better. The movement reminded him of something and, almost involuntarily, his left arm curled up into the air. Feeling foolish, he brought the arm back in, but when he looked down—and much to his surprise— he caught his shoe tracing an arc in the dust of Emerald's parking lot.

Greg

Greg Cullen had a date with destiny. He knew he did because as soon as he had made it back to his room from helping his father bring some junk into the house, his song had come on. He went to the mirror. He bowed, then struck a pose. He held it for a few seconds, then struck a second pose. He took in deep breaths. He stayed centered. He was doing it like the book said. The book, which he had purchased two days prior in Frankfort, detailed the sacred fundamentals of wushu. He had already explained to his best friend, Sugar, that wushu was the real name for kung fu. It was more ancient and more important. The author's name was Bill Blankenship. Bill Blankenship had studied with a verified master.

Greg dropped his right leg back, crouched, hunched his shoulders, and threw a punch. Bruce Lee looked down at him from a poster on one wall. Chuck Norris from the other. Sugar liked Chuck, and Greg liked Bruce. Sugar had gotten his nickname because he had done some boxing and had always knocked Greg around when they got to it, but now Greg had found wushu. Or wushu had found Greg. Greg threw another punch and made a low kick. He wasn't sure he had gotten the kick right. He couldn't tell if the kick was meant to be low or midrange. The picture in the book was a little unclear. The pictures were all in black-and-white. Greg wished they were color. He thought that if they were in color he could see them more clearly. Black-and-white made things seems blurry. When the song ended, Greg flicked his chin at Chuck and bowed to Bruce. He wished they would just play his song again, but he knew he would have to wait. Still, that it had come on when it did really meant something. He thought about calling Sugar up to tell him about it, but it was Thursday and Thursday meant Sugar was already at work, just like Greg would be in less than an hour, so instead he lay down on his bed.

Greg had a waterbed. His father had bought two, one for himself and one for Greg, at a fire sale a few years ago. He had been able to afford them because the heating units had something wrong with them. Greg's father kept promising to look into it, but he hadn't even set up his own yet and probably never would. Now it was summer so it didn't matter, but in the winter the water in the bed got very cold. Sometimes in the summer Greg's father came and slept on the bed with him to stay cool. It was a big bed, so there was plenty of room. Sugar slept on the bed too when he stayed all night. No one got seasick because the bed had built-in baffles. The salesman had smacked the demo unit to show that there were no ripples. He had had both Greg and his father smack the bed. Smacking the bed in the shop had been satisfying. Greg's father had been very happy the day they brought the beds home. There was some mess when they filled Greg's up with the hose and a small leak needed patching and Greg's father swore a great deal. Greg liked it when his father swore. He was good at it. He said he'd learned everything he knew about swearing on the tennis court back when he was runner-up champ or something in high school. Greg had started the day off by reading magazines, and a pile lay on one side of the mattress. Greg's father called this the passenger side. Sometimes he called it the bed's sidecar. Greg stretched his arm out and lay the back of his hand on the magazines. They were cool like the bed, and the back of his hand and wrist stuck to them. The magazines were mostly about three-wheelers and martial arts. Greg was pretty much too old to want a three-wheeler anymore, but he still liked to look at three-wheeler magazines. At first he had wanted a Honda ATC110, and then he had wanted a Honda ATC185. Most of the pictures in his magazines had been taken in California. For a few months last year Sugar had had a Suzuki three-wheeler stored in his old barn. It never worked, but they both sat on it and on the dead tractor beside it quite a bit.

Now Greg was saving up for a car. Greg's father had offered him his Pinto, but Greg didn't want anything to do with that barfy piece of crap. Greg had his eye on something with some engine to it. Sugar already had his permit. They talked a lot about cars. Sometimes they talked about girls, but mostly it was about cars and martial arts. Sugar's thing about boxing was that he had a second cousin who ran a gym over in Kokomo. Sugar went there on weekends sometimes. Also he had a heavy bag in his barn and could do ten thousand pushups and jumped rope pretty well. Sugar's second cousin had won a tournament up in Fort Wayne supposedly. Greg didn't have any cousins who had won tournaments. There was one who was much older

and served catfish over at Miller's in Colfax and another he'd
never met who did something with birds or lizards at the Indianapolis Zoo, but that wasn't the kind of thing that could help you.
Not in the game of life. Greg's new book would help though.
He wished the pictures were better, but they were okay. You got
the general idea. Bill Blankenship's master had studied with a
master of his own all the way over in Taiwan. Greg had looked
Taiwan up in the atlas. He thought it would be nice to have a
master. He'd had coaches but never a master. Greg's feet were
about as flat as pancakes and he was terrible at basketball, but
wushu didn't care how high your arches were.

Greg unstuck his hand and wrist from the magazine without
tearing it and stood up. He wondered when he would start
groaning when he stood up. His father said probably it would be
a while. That the fewer sports you played when you were young
the later you would start to groan, but Greg wasn't sure. He had
teachers who had never played sports who weren't that old and
groaned like maniacs. There was another song on now that
wasn't bad. In general, Greg liked slower songs with a lot of bass
to them. He liked it when there were long instrumentals as well
as a story in the song. Sugar liked heavy metal and Greg did too,
but when he was alone he liked things to run a little slower, a
little softer. It didn't matter if the story didn't have anything to
do with him. Or if he couldn't entirely understand what the story
was about. Greg bowed and struck his pose. He could hear his
father's Pinto rattling away down the driveway. His father was
taking Turder Davis to get flowers. Turder was what Greg and
Sugar called Turner Davis, a retired janitor, behind his back.

Greg didn't like the old names. He liked names like
Michael, Kevin, Amy, Michelle, John, Rich, Kim, Brian, Tina,
Greg, and Tod. Names like Turner, Myrtle, Wilma, Ethel,

Emerson, Winnifred, Virgil, Ruby, and Zorrie made him feel like he had tripped at the cemetery and couldn't stand back up, like the skeleton with the scythe was getting ready to impale him or at least put him in a joint lock. Greg made two kicks to keep the feeling at bay. He could already tell that wushu would be good for things like that. He bowed. He decided that he would keep his green headband on when he went to work. The headband made him feel focused. It was made out of his gym shirt. He had cut and tied it very carefully. He wondered if there were some symbols to do with wushu that he could write on it. He thought about punching Sugar and then kicking him. Later he would definitely show Sugar what he could do.

Greg left his room, locked the door behind him, then went downstairs and made himself a sandwich. After he had put away the mayonnaise and mustard, he got them back out and made a second sandwich for his father. He put a pair of Kraft singles on his father's sandwich to go with the bologna. Greg's father sometimes forgot to eat. Greg knew he would come in the kitchen when he got back because that's where his soda was. Greg's father drank soda all damn day and all damn night. He bought it in the big bottles and by the case and said he got indigestion if he didn't have it. Greg surrounded his father's sandwich with chips and put some in a bag for himself. The chips were plain. Greg would have preferred ranch or barbecue flavor, but a boring chip was better than no chip. Plain was probably what Bill Blankenship would have recommended anyway. Maybe he said something about eating in the wushu way later in the book. Greg would read some more of it after work. When he leaned down to grab the handle of his Igloo cooler, the back of his headband fell over his left shoulder. He wondered if he ought to cut it shorter. He liked it long but thought it could get annoying. Greg remembered that his favorite song had come on right when he had hoped it would. Days when that happened were special. It was like when things happened in the Bible or in the movies. He loaded up his cooler and left the house.

There had been wind and thunder the night before, but now it was nice out. Greg's father had always said Greg was sensitive to the weather. He said Greg took after his mother in this way. Sometimes, when Greg was little, the three of them had watched episodes of *Kung Fu* with David Carradine. They had all sat close together. In one episode, David Carradine's character, Caine, practiced shooting arrows in the dark. He would take aim, draw the arrow back, and then look away as he released it. Greg's mother laughed a lot while they watched. She said that David Carradine wasn't even half Chinese like Caine was supposed to be and that nobody in real life ever talked like that. Greg didn't care. He bet Bill Blankenship had seen that episode. Greg took aim with an imaginary arrow at a pair of mourning doves sitting on the electric wire. The heavy, insulated wire drooped low so that part of it had been swallowed by the old pear tree. The front lawn needed to be mowed. Greg wondered where you could buy an actual wushu bow. Maybe you could make one. Terry Royer was in his driveway down the street practicing placekicking with a Mountain Dew can. Greg was late for work or he might have joined in. Terry was four years younger than him. Both Terry's parents had good jobs over in Kokomo. They had tried to help Greg's father get a job, but it hadn't worked out. If Sugar wasn't around, Greg sometimes played Atari with Terry on their sectional couch. They had central air and a cupboard full of snacks. They had a dog that had something wrong with it and couldn't bark. Terry's mother drove a yellow Mustang, and his father owned a nice truck. They took a lot of trips. Terry had

T-shirts from five different states. Greg wondered if Terry wasn't in some way wrapped up in his good fortune. He had thought about shooting him with his imaginary wushu bow but instead— after Terry tried to hit him with the can and Greg blocked it with his cooler—he demonstrated a double punch, shot one imaginary arrow up into the sky, and then bowed.

"What's with the karate?" Terry asked.

"It's not karate, it's something better. I'm going to kick Sugar's ass with it."

Greg walked past the library. It was a small stone building built back when everyone's name was Elmira and Homer or something stupid like that. There were bushy evergreens on either side of the front steps, and he and Sugar had used to hide behind them and yell back and forth in a secret language at each other. They had spent a lot of time on the secret language. Greg liked the library. You could check out cassettes, and there was a book in the sports section written by a former marine about jiujitsu. Greg had read it closely but didn't have much no interest in jiujitsu. He hated anything that was like wrestling. He had done wrestling in gym class too many times to count. Every time you wrestled you had to put on a singlet. Wushu was completely different. Wushu was a part of life. It was just natural. You didn't need to wear any kind of crotch-hugging special suit. You could if you wanted, but you didn't have to.

Work was right up the street. Everything was nearby. Greg could have gone home during his break, but he never did anymore. A time or two when he had gone home on his break, he had found his father sleeping on the waterbed. The first time, Greg's father had jumped up off the bed and seemed embarrassed to be sleeping there in the middle of the day. The second time he had stayed sleeping. Greg's break was only twenty minutes anyway. Sugar had a job bagging groceries at the Marsh in Frankfort and was always taking long breaks. Sugar was the youngest one who worked there, and to hear him tell it nobody cared what he did as long as he showed up. This was Greg's third year at the Galaxy Swirl. He worked almost full time in the summer and every other weekend in the spring.

When Greg got there, Della Dorner was fussing with the soft-serve machine. She started laughing at his headband before he had even gotten in the door. Greg set down his cooler, stood up straight, and assumed an attitude of calm. He told Della his headband was a "mark of the way," which was a phrase used by Bill Blankenship to describe the things that came along with you on your journey.

"Of the say who what now?" Della said.

Della was nominally Greg's supervisor, but they mostly just both did the bare minimum and spent a lot of time horsing around. Della had changed since last summer though. She looked different. Greg was finally taller than her, but now she had her braces off and plus she had big boobs. Back in the spring, Greg had heard Terry Royer's mom telling someone on the phone that Della Dorner was developing into a real "doll baby." Greg and Della were the same age and had always gone to school together. Della's mom worked at the hospital. Her grandfather was a retired sheriff. Nobody messed with him. She talked about going to college and had been to Florida twice. Greg thought of bowing at Della but instead he flipped her off. Della returned the favor, only she did it with both hands. Della's hands had grown along with her boobs, leaving her fingers disconcertingly long. Greg was always afraid she would want to compare hand size. Sugar made fun of Greg's hands, although his own were only slightly bigger.

"Stock the drink fridge, my slave," Della said.

"Stock it yourself," Greg responded.

But it was an even day, and on even days the drink fridge was Greg's responsibility.

"We're low on DPs," Della said, taking on a brisk, business-like tone.

"Yeah, yeah," said Greg.

"Shed's unlocked."

"Whatever."

According to Bill Blankenship, part of the wushu way was to let yourself be guided in all things and at all moments by your inner vision, so Greg went out to the storage shed with his eyes closed. He kept his hands clasped behind his back so that he couldn't cheat. Bill Blankenship had said that true sight took years to attain, but Greg was a fast learner. He and his father had gone to see *Star Wars* six times, and he thought of Luke in his X-wing starfighter when, after eight firm steps, he unclasped his hands and brought one of them around to reach for what he felt sure would be the door knob. He knew that if he doubted even for a moment, the knob wouldn't be where his inner vision told him it was. Sometimes in his room he tried to push his hand straight through the molecules of the wall. He knew that he could do it if he didn't doubt, but he always doubted. The world was an illusion. With his eyes closed he could feel his other senses come alive. In this way he was like Daredevil. Greg wondered what it would be like to be truly blind. He thought he would be good at it. That, like Daredevil, he probably wouldn't need a special stick even if, for appearances, he carried one. Luke wouldn't have needed a special stick either. Greg brought his hand in at what he thought would be an effective angle. Maybe it was a vector instead of an angle. His hand was like the torpedo launched from Luke's fighter. At the last second, he torqued his hand and pulled his thumb and index finger firmly apart, and the patch of skin between them landed directly on its target. Greg wondered if that patch of skin had a name. It was kind of like the armpit of his hand. That sounded stupid. Keeping his eyes closed, he pulled open the door. He was trying to decide if he would grab up the case of Dr. Peppers and carry them back without opening his eyes, when one of Della's big, slender hands smacked him hard between the shoulder blades.

It didn't bother Greg that Della had taken advantage of his dedication to his training to knock him onto his knees and—before he could reorient himself and get up—lock him in the shed. Nor did it much bother him that it was so dark. Bill Blankenship and Bill Blankenship's master and Bill Blankenship's master's master would of course have sensed anyone, friend or foe, attempting to come up behind them even in the middle of a training exercise. With time, Greg too would be able to calmly turn at the last second and, without opening his eyes, quickly but gently block the strike of his attacker and waggle his index finger dismissively at her. Indeed, Greg bet that if they were to do it again, right now, if there could be a do-over, his heightened senses would detect Della not just as she sneaked behind him on the short path to the shed but even as she made the decision to come out after him in the first place. Thoughts were very loud, according to Bill Blankenship, and Greg believed that the next time Della had one that concerned him he would sense it and react accordingly. His inner light had led him without hesitation to the door handle, and there were many other things that light could do.

Greg felt sure of it. He imagined that by the time they returned to school in the fall, he would be able to walk easily through the crowded hallways with his eyes closed. He would be able to drive with his eyes closed. He would kick Sugar's ass with his eyes closed. Terry Royer could watch. Terry might cheer, but Greg wouldn't care about that. A wushu warrior didn't require applause. A wushu warrior served a higher purpose and was a servant of the collective destiny. Maybe he would teach Terry the wushu way. They could travel throughout central Indiana together. Greg could start a school. Together, he and Terry, when Terry was ready, could found a dynasty. It was important to have students. He would be Terry's master. Greg was happy that Della had pushed him. It had made him think about important things. Her big hand had made a sharp, loud sound as it had hit the skin between his shoulders. It had felt and sounded like a little belly flop. Greg had always been known for his cannonballs at the pool. Sugar had always specialized in jackknifes. Now that Greg was following the wushu way, he would probably get into flips. He tried without much luck to picture doing a flip with his eyes closed.

Greg sat down on the stack of soda cases and wondered how long Della was going to keep him locked in the shed. The Galaxy Swirl would open soon. It was always slow at first and then it got busier. Some days they could barely keep up. Greg could actually see a little. There was a rectangle of light around the shed door. He truly wasn't very bothered by the dark. Once his mother had shut him in the basement, but it hadn't been for long. His father had come home and heard him yelling. Greg had had a choice between the basement and getting his mouth washed out with soap. His mother sat him down and explained, in no small detail, the pros and cons of each scenario. Greg chose the basement, then after a little while down there he changed his mind. He was sobbing about wanting the soap when his father came home. *Sobbing* was the word Greg heard his father use on the phone later. Greg's mother had left a long time ago. She had been very funny. Everyone said so when she came up. "No shit, Sherlock!" and "How's come, honeypie?" were the kinds of things she had been known to say. It had been all about the timing. Greg's father almost always smiled when Greg said something about her.

Greg's father's teeth had once been very white. You could see it in his old yearbooks. Greg's mother had smiled with her mouth closed. At least for school pictures. The fact of the matter was you never knew what someone's teeth were going to be like until they opened their mouths. His mother had been on the JV cheer squad but had gotten cut from varsity. Just like Greg with basketball. Greg wondered how big his mother's hands had been. There were still some of her shoes in one of the closets. They were not too big and not too small. Greg liked fairy tales. He would have solved the problem of Goldilocks by shooting the two bigger bears one by one with his wushu bow as they came through the front door. Greg didn't care about his flat feet, but he wished his hands were bigger. Maybe they would still grow. That remained a possibility. Greg's father liked to say that most things usually worked themselves out and that if they didn't you would be dead soon enough anyway. Greg's father liked to call himself an optimist, but sometimes Greg could hear him crying at night.

There was just one thing that troubled Greg about his situation. It was that Della had somehow removed his headband when she shoved him. He hadn't felt her do it and hadn't realized it at first. This meant that not only had Della taken advantage of his intense concentration during the training exercise to sneak up on him, she had also reached out with her long fingers and lifted up the part of his headband that hung down between his shoulders. Without his knowing it, Della had reached out and she had grabbed the green cloth and then she had smacked him on the back. It really had sounded like a belly flop. It had hurt like one too. Greg should have followed his instinct and cut the tail off his headband before he came to work. Not doing so had been an error. Knowing Della she would be wearing it. Once she had yanked his Pacers cap off his head and put it on hers. But then again that was when they were younger. Before everything got complicated. Maybe she had just tossed his headband in the trash.

Greg knew Della knew he looked at her boobs. Sometimes she complained about them giving her a backache and so forth, but it didn't ever sound like she meant it. For one thing they weren't that big. Beryl Reedy, Sugar's supervisor at the Marsh, had the really big ones. They were easily twice as big as Della's. Greg had known Della forever. He wondered what she was doing. Probably she was fussing some more with the soft-serve machine or doing the final check and thinking about how she would lord this over him for the next one hundred thousand years. Very soon it would be time to get the music going. They always started playing music ten minutes before opening. It was the same station Greg listened to when he was alone. Once or twice his song had come on at work. No one, not even Sugar, knew that it was Greg's song. Della had asked Greg to dance with her at the seventh grade Halloween social. He had turned her down. He had not been very nice to her about it. In fact he had spit tropical punch in her face. Not too much but a little. Enough. He was glad seventh grade was years ago now. Maybe he would tell Della about his song. Greg wanted his headband back. Taking it had been adding insult to injury. He had lost honor. A man had to chart his own course of action, but Greg wondered what Bill Blankenship would do.

Greg could hear cars going by on Main. He could hear a lawnmower over at Horace Allen's. Horace was another name he didn't like. He liked Horace though. Horace had always been nice to him. He knew his father sometimes borrowed money from Horace, and he also knew that Horace never got mad about it. Greg's father said Horace had learned patience among other things during the war. Greg could hear cardinals and robins. At least he thought that was what they were. Someone yelled over in the direction of Cubby Rogers's garage. It sounded like they were saying something about backing up. The garage was a hundred yards away. Greg had known since the moment he had pushed himself up off his knees, found his balance, and pivoted in the dark to face his attacker, Della Beth Dorner, that he would probably be heard if he yelled. He was in no way trapped. Also if he had to, he could knock the door down. The door was hollow. It had been broken into before. At the end of each shift, he and Della put the padlock on, but during the day it was just a handle lock. Della could have put the padlock on, but she hadn't. That would have been taking the joke too far. Sugar never said anything when Greg talked about Della. Greg thought women needed to be respected. What Sugar needed was his ass kicked, and Greg was just the man for the job. Della ought to have shoved Sugar into the shed, not him. Greg practiced throwing punches in the dark. Probably he could punch as well as kick through the door if he needed to. A wushu warrior didn't damage things unnecessarily though. A wushu warrior's greatest weapon was patience.

Greg closed his eyes and took a deep breath. Sitting on the soda cases with his eyes closed in the almost dark of the shed, it seemed to Greg after maybe about half a minute that he was somewhere else. It was a strange feeling, like waking up in the middle of the night at a sleepover and not knowing where you were, only that you'd just wet the bed. Bill Blankenship wrote about how it was in "the calm within the calm" that we find our true power. Maybe that was what this was. Maybe Greg had found his true power, maybe that was what his song had been telling him. It was a great fucking song. One for the ages. Greg's father liked Steely Dan. Steely Dan made Greg want to puke. Steely Dan was butt chunks. He took a deep breath. He kept his eyes closed. He was no longer in the shed. But where was he? He thought maybe he could see water. A small blue pool sparkling and lapping in front of him. It looked a little like the pool in Frankfort where he did his cannonballs. Or maybe it was a lake. He had gone to Indiana Beach one time with his mother. His mother had taken him up there in the Pinto for the day while his father was at work. In the end his father had had to take a bus up so he could drive them home. Greg's mother had wanted to go waterskiing, but Greg was too small, so she rented a canoe. She hadn't been happy about it and wasn't very good at paddling. The lake seemed very big. Greg could remember her singing. It was hard to tell what the water was. Maybe it wasn't even water. For a second it seemed like he was back in his room, back on his bed. His bed was made of water so that made sense. He was lying on it with his hand and wrist on the magazines. He had the magazines because for a while his father had gotten into selling subscriptions and you could have your own for a discount. After Greg's mother had left, she lived in Frankfort for a while and sold advertising spots for Shine 99. Before the radio in the Pinto had stopped pulling in anything besides static, Greg's father listened to that station a lot.

Greg wondered when Della would put the music on. It seemed like she should have done it already. If she had, he would have heard it because there was a speaker for the side tables next to the shed. Greg could see quite a bit now once his eyes were open again. He could easily read the sign on the back of the door that said "Don't Forget to Log Whatever Comes Out and Whatever Comes In!!!" There were actually four exclamation points, but one of them had faded. Greg told himself he would count to one hundred and if Della hadn't come back before he had finished, he would break open the door. Greg started out counting Mississippis, then, figuring that was too boring, switched to chimpanzees. Greg had a soft spot for chimpanzees. Whenever he and his father went down to see their cousin at the Indianapolis Zoo, Greg always looked in on them.

Horace

Horace Allen could smell the sea. It spilled in through the window, crawled along the floor, inched up and over the bed. Because his house stood something like seven hundred miles from saltwater, and many thousands of miles from the saltwater he had in mind, this was a sea conjured by memory and the conjoined smell of thyme, oregano, sage, marjoram, basil, tomato plant, and cucumber vine. A sea that came alive every clear morning now as soon as the sun hit his herb pots and window planters. Horace sighed contentedly and let the remembered water take him. Cover everything but his face. The sea was cool but not cold. The sun began to grow hot on his cheeks. He knew there were small, silver fish all around him. In a moment he would flip himself over and swim after them.

On a good morning, as this one had been, Horace carried the sea with him for a while when he got out of bed. He wore it like a glittering cape as he made his coffee, as he crunched his toast, as he listened to the news and weather, as he considered what lay ahead. Horace liked to know what the day had in store. He liked to size it up and give it some shape. Used to be, before he had retired from farming, Horace would have upward of twenty-five things written down on a yellow ledger. The only ledger he kept now was in his head. Today the main thing was he had to mow.

The sea began to fall away from Horace as he thought about mowing. It was gone by the time he put his dishes in the sink and grabbed his hat and went outside. He held his breath as he passed his planters. He didn't want to spoil things by smelling them again too soon. It had taken him years to find the right combination. It was only when Jodi Davis had offered him a spare oregano plant that it had all fallen into place. He had not known it would bring the distant sea back to him so vividly. He had wept the first time it returned.

Horace's gas can gave out only the sorriest slosh. Filling it up would come first thing. He went ahead and pulled the mower out of the shed so the sun could warm it. It always started with one pull when it was warm. Horace was a John Deere man. He had paid extra to have the best model. The salesman in Frankfort said it would run for years. Every now and again he'd soak the plugs and that was about it. He had plenty of oil on hand. It was just the gas he was short on. The filling station attached to Cubby Rogers's garage opened at seven. He'd walk over. If he took the long way, he would hit it just about the time Cubby was switching on the pumps.

So he went right on Nebraska instead of left and marched up the quiet street and turned left on Truman and crossed Main. Both Jodi and Turner Davis were out in Jodi's garden. Jodi was barking orders and Turner was following them. They both stopped and waved when they saw him. Turner asked him how he was coming. Horace held up his gas can and gave it a wiggle. Even this early in the season, Jodi's garden was a thing to inspire awe. Horace could imagine someone using it as the subject of a sermon. The rest of the yard, which was Turner's domain, hadn't quite hit its stride.

Horace went past Iowa, then turned left on Archer. It was a fine, bright morning. It was pleasant to be out walking after a storm. His leg never hurt much in the summer. As he went by, Myrtle Kelly waved at him out the big window of her front room. For a while after her husband had passed, they had kept each other company, but it hadn't worked out. It hadn't worked out for Horace with anyone.

There had been quite a few in the community over the years who had been soft on him. Horace had always gone easy on the eyes, and old as he was getting, this was still true. Time wasn't in any great hurry with him was the way Myrtle had put it. He wasn't especially tall, but he was naturally lean, didn't sweat too much, and looked good in a pressed cotton shirt. Like Gary Cooper but shorter, Alma Dunn had once said. He had taken her on three dates. She had gotten pretty worked up about things. He hadn't married her or anyone else though. For a while there had been whispers of the nasty variety, but they hadn't stuck. There hadn't been anything for them to stick to.

Horace whistled a little as he walked down along Archer with the empty gas can. He was not much of a whistler, but he engaged in the practice frequently. He had played trombone in his high school orchestra. That had pleased him even more, though he had not been much better at it than he was at whistling. In the army they had let him tap the triangle and bang the cymbals with an orchestra all the way up until D-Day. Horace did not like to think about D-Day. Both the cornet and piano players had been blown to pieces beside him on Omaha Beach. As he was whistling his way around the bend onto Adams, Hank Dunn's granddaughter came tearing down her driveway and almost ran into him. When she hollered out, "Sorry, Mr. Allen!" over her shoulder, the sun caught the back of her head and turned her light-brown hair into gold. As she flew off down the street with a grin on her face, her hair stayed golden and, for a moment, Horace, who had left himself vulnerable with his careless thoughts of Normandy, came undone.

HE HAD FOUGHT on after D-Day until only the violinist was left alive, and then he, too, had been killed. The war had ended for Horace at the Battle of Nancy, which he had survived only because a friend had managed to drag him far enough out of the Moselle that at least he wouldn't drown. He wasn't well enough to move for six weeks, and it was only after the fall of Berlin that he was allowed to leave the hospital. After a few months, a captain he'd had a hand in evacuating before his own wounding put in a word, and a half year after the conclusion of the war in Europe, Horace was given permission to travel. He went first to the south of France, then to Corsica, where he fell in with a pair of Australian survivors of the Battle of Crete. They had made it to Egypt when the island fell, but many of their fellows had been left behind, and they wanted to go back now and spit on what was left of the Führer's boots.

After a few days spent in a crumbling hotel that looked out onto a bomb-damaged mosque across the harbor in the city of Chania, Horace and his companions had made their way inland. They were traveling in uniform, and everywhere they stopped, the Cretans poured them small glasses of the local brandy. Horace had drunk almost nothing during the war, but he accepted the glasses with a smile. In the ruins of a village called Anogia, amid all the dark hair and bright, fierce eyes, he caught a glimpse of blonde spilling out of a black headscarf. When the Australians pressed on for Hora Sfakia, where the evacuation had occurred, though not before many of the men around them had been "butchered like goats," Horace stayed behind.

She offered him only her given name, Rose-Alice. Her mother was American and her father a Scottish archaeologist who had overseen excavations in Crete before the war. Horace did not ask her what she was doing there, dressed in dark cloth and living in a ruined village, but when he talked to her—beside a shared water spigot, then at the mouth of an alleyway leading away from the town's square—he felt something come back to life in him. One evening there was dancing under the trees. Horace did not join in, but he clapped his hands on the offbeat as he had been instructed and watched Rose-Alice as she held hands with others and moved back and forth, arms raised, in the line. Their eyes met several times during this dancing. A sheep had been roasted. No one knew just where it had been procured, though many wore knowing smiles. Horace chewed small pieces of meat seasoned with thyme and oregano. Sometimes men at the end of the lines made spectacular jumps that Horace appreciated but didn't understand.

The next day, early, Rose-Alice was waiting for him when he came out of the small house on the edge of the village where he had been given a room. There was a truck going down to the sea. She didn't ask him if he wanted to accompany her. There was no need. They rode down in a jumble of old sheep pelts and swam for hours in a turquoise bay. Rose-Alice had packed a lunch of cheese, stuffed peppers, and barley rusks that she soaked in the glittering bay. On the way back up, the load in the truck had changed from soft to hard and they were forced to sit close. Their shoulders touched so many times with the truck's constant jostling that they gave up trying to keep apart.

Both of them smelled like the water they had had such a hard time leaving behind. Horace kept sniffing his fingers, his shirt, his forearms. Rose-Alice said it was the smell of Greece, that there wasn't anything like it anywhere else in the world. She hadn't been able to get all of her damp hair stuffed back into the scarf. Horace did his best not to look directly at her when she talked.

After a time, Horace told Rose-Alice as they rode along that he wasn't scared. He blurted this out and it surprised him. Usually, he kept such things to himself. He had been scared for a very long time but he wasn't anymore and this seemed remarkable to him. Rose-Alice reached out and touched his hand when he said this. Touched it very lightly. And as they rode the rest of the way in silence, Horace took the fancy that a tree or a flower might bloom up from the spot. A woman was waiting by the little church where the truck dropped them. She didn't say anything, just took Rose-Alice by the elbow and led her away.

The next morning Rose-Alice was waiting for Horace again. This time they didn't go down to the sea. Instead, after taking him for a short ride in an abandoned German jeep, she led him up the lower slopes of Mt. Psiloritis to the mouth of the cave where Zeus was said to have been born and to have hid so that the mad god who was his father wouldn't find and kill him. It was a beautiful spot. A great plain stretched below and they could see for miles. Just outside the cave there was a grave covered in white rocks.

As they walked down the slope and then rode back to the village, Rose-Alice told him that the resident of the grave, her husband, had been part of the resistance during the German invasion of the island. That she had come to know him before the war when he had helped on her father's digs. That she had stayed behind after the evacuation, during which she had volunteered in the Red Cross, because she heard he had been wounded somewhere up in the hills. That she had made it up to where he lay, barely conscious, just before he died. That the woman Horace had seen the night before, her dead husband's sister, was helping her to keep her own promise. That both of them came once each week to pray beside his grave. That she would never—and she looked long and carefully at Horace when she said this—leave Crete.

She touched his hand again just before they returned to Anogia. Horace did not think about trees and flowers this time. Two men with thick black moustaches and bright blue eyes were waiting for him. They were not unkind. Both of them had been among those who had made great jumps during the dancing under the trees and both had offered him glasses of spirits that night and toasted his health. Rose-Alice stood completely still with her arms across her chest as they all three got in a truck to take him back to Chania. Horace thought he heard her say, "Goodbye, Mr. Allen," but he wasn't quite sure. He never saw her again.

Hank Dunn's granddaughter vanished around a corner. Horace knew she was on the track team. That she was a better-than-fair quarter miler and ran anchor on the JV relay team. The morning light swallowed her completely. Rose-Alice had run

ahead of him down to the beach. She had called out to him over
her shoulder. She had yelled, "Come on, Mr. Allen!" Then as
now his leg hadn't allowed him to run. Usually when the past
took him unexpectedly—when he hadn't called it forth by
concoction of smells or careless thought—it did so in the middle
of dark dreams. This time had been different. It amazed Horace
how different it had been.

WHEN HE GOT home, he gassed up the mower, double-checked
the oil, then took a walk around his front, side, and back yards to
pick up any sticks and branches that might have fallen during
the storm. It hadn't been all that much of a storm, more a light-
show than anything else as far as he could tell, but there had been
some good wind by the end of it, and the shag hickory had
given up long curving pieces of bark, and the persimmon had
thrown down half a dozen twigs from one of its elegantly
overgrown arms. There were leaves, too, scattered here and
there but not enough to get worked up about.

When he got over to the crabapple, the robin whose kingdom
it was began to scold him, and he saw that there was an egg
caught in the cushiony grass at his feet. The egg shone very blue
against the surrounding grass. Horace picked it up, saw that it
was intact, felt that it was still warm, then reached up and, with
the outraged robin leaping from branch to branch above, carefully tucked it back into her nest. Probably it was too late but
maybe it wasn't. He hoped not.

Horace walked over to the house and leaned in close to the
kitchen window until he could see the clock on the wall next to
the refrigerator. It was still too early to mow. Ethel Goodwin
next door had a summer cold and would still be asleep. In the

countryside you could start work whenever you wanted, but in town you had to wait. Horace had worked the family farm for more than thirty years before selling and moving into town. On the farm there had always been something that needed his attention. Even when there wasn't you could make something up. He had usually started his days at five.

How he had loved to go out to the barn in the dark! Sometimes he had screamed at the stars as he walked across the yard. He had screamed for his dead fellows. He had screamed for himself. Sometimes they had been screams of joy. He didn't understand this anymore than he had the leaps of the dancers on Crete, but it was true. There was a lot that he didn't really understand. For a long time he had collected all the white or whitish rocks he had plowed or dug up and made a pile of them out behind the barn.

Where had Hank Dunn's granddaughter been going? Why had she been smiling? Horace had heard from Hank that she had placed at Sectionals that year. Or had it even been Regionals? A cardinal was chirping to its mate about some food it had found. The day's warmth was starting to really set in. Indiana in July was very beautiful. "This is a day that the Lord hath made," Horace said aloud. It was what his mother had whispered to him as they hugged when, well into 1945, he finally came home.

He had never told anyone about Crete. He wondered if he had ever even said the name Rose-Alice aloud. He must have said it to her at the very least, but he couldn't remember doing so. Why was he thinking about this? About her? It was so rare now that he did. Of course, she came into his mind fairly often but that was different than thinking about her. What after half a whole lifetime was there to think about?

Hank Dunn's granddaughter had been like a jack-in-the-box. Like a stick of dynamite. Well, not like that. He did not do well with explosions. Not even on the Fourth. Stick of dynamite was just something Hank Dunn liked to say. Rose-Alice had run beautifully too. He wondered if she had ever raced anyone. Perhaps she and the Phoenix had raced. At one of her father's digs before the war. Where was God and his days in all this? When his parents died, he had stopped going to church. He still sometimes picked up the Bible though. He was not against any of it. Sometimes he had gone out to the pile of white rocks and bowed his head.

WHEN HE STARTED to see signs of life over at Ethel Goodwin's, Horace pulled the mower away from the shed and onto the grass. He found it started even more easily than he thought it would. It started with barely half a pull. It really was a good machine. Horace loved following it around the yard. For a moment he held the handle steady, let the vibration travel through his hands and up his arms to meet between his shoulders. Then he pulled up on the safety mechanism and engaged the blades. There was very little else, for Horace, like the opening whir of a mower's blade.

He worked slowly, carefully, stopping from time to time to fetch up a stick he had missed on his earlier sweep. Time passed while he mowed, but he had a different sense of it. It passed in the little pieces of grass that found their way onto the backs of his hands. It passed in the muscles and hair and sweat of his forearms. It passed in the changing smell of the oil and the gasoline as the two-stroke engine got deep into its work. It passed in the sound of that small, hardworking machine. It passed in the rising temperature of the air, in the whipping by of birds, in the floating of clouds. It passed in his feet getting hot in his boots. In his lower back getting sore. The pain in his back was connected to the old injury. Injury wasn't quite the right word for what had happened to him, but he used it if someone he didn't know very well remarked on his limp. There had been big dead fish—not pretty little silver ones—floating in the eddies of the Moselle River around him when he was pulled out.

Horace liked to rake after he had completed each section of his yard. The rake was like a metronome. The earth was like a clock. The smell of the grass as the sturdy bamboo tines moved through it made him think of overripe apples. The grass didn't smell like overripe apples. The smell just made him think of them. The mower rested while he raked. Horace could almost hear it panting, like it was catching its breath, trying to cool off. Sometimes, after he had been mowing for a while, say after he had finished two sections of the yard, it seemed like all he had to do was blow on the machine and it would leap back to life, like the actual pulling wasn't even necessary, was just an afterthought.

Horace leaned the rake against the shed, went into the house and got himself a drink. The municipal water was not as cool as he would have liked, but it was wet. This was something Myrtle Kelly had often said about the water at her own house. Myrtle had been full of expressions and funny remarks. She had a loud laugh. She was good company. Sometimes in the summertime they still sat on her front steps at noon and ate chipped beef or egg salad sandwiches together.

Horace thought of Myrtle waving at him earlier and then of sitting next to her on the front steps. She had long since stopped taking his hand and pulling it over onto her knee. They were just

friends now. She hadn't held any grudge. Suddenly a visit with
Myrtle and her big laugh sounded nice. Like it might be just the
thing. He surveyed the back yard from the kitchen window. The
grass was springing back up, and he could see where he had
missed a few spots.

Horace took another drink of the tap-warm water. He had
had a pump on the farm and had frequently stuck his head under
it. Glory, the water on his farm had been cold! Sometimes over
the years, when he had gotten into thinking that if he had
somehow done things differently it might not just have been the
one trip with Rose-Alice down to the bay, he had put his head
under the pump. The pump had always cleared his thinking
straight away.

Ethel Goodwin was sitting on her porch swing with a wash-
cloth covering her face. When Horace called out a greeting, she
lifted up a hand then let it, autumn-leaf-like, sort of sing itself
back down. Toby Slocum was out on Main with his Ronald
Reagan sign. Reagan had been president for more than two
years, but Toby still liked to walk up and down Main with his
sign like the campaign was still on. Sometimes cars honked. This
pleased Toby greatly. As Horace crossed Main, someone yelled
something encouraging at Toby out the window of a purple
Impala. Toby held up his sign and beamed. When he saw Horace,
he waved. Horace nodded back, afraid that if he held up one of
the sodas he'd grabbed out of the fridge to share with Myrtle,
Toby might think he was offering it to him. Not that he would
have begrudged Toby a soda. Horace liked Toby. Plus he had
money in the bank and sodas to share. It was just that it might
have been confusing. Toby wasn't dumb exactly, or even at all,
but he did confuse easy. His cardboard was looking a little
floppy. Probably it had been held too tightly and sweat on too

much. For a long time, Toby had carried a Jesus sign around, but now it was Reagan. Horace supposed that in a year or two he would be on to someone else.

Myrtle had been big on Jesus for a while. She had talked about him quite a bit, like he was a brother or someone she had known in high school, a very good friend, but then one day she had just stopped. She was like that. Horace had teared up the day he had told her he couldn't keep coming over anymore. At least not in the same way. Myrtle had laughed and kissed him on the cheek and said he was almost as cute when he got teary-eyed as he was when he smiled.

All was well now though, and he was overdue for a visit. Horace tucked one of the cold sodas under his arm and knocked on her door. He was about to lift his hand again when he remembered that it was the third Thursday of the month, that Myrtle had club today. It wasn't club time yet, but Myrtle always had lunch with one of the girls before heading over for an afternoon of fun.

Horace laughed at himself for having forgotten. He didn't usually do that. He turned and looked down off Myrtle's front porch, past the steps and out to the street. He had always liked this view. If you squinted, you could see all the way to the fields past town. Right now, with the sun directly overhead and the heat shimmering slightly on the street, the fields were just a smear of green, smudged here and there with brown. When he walked over past the kitchen window to the edge of Myrtle's porch to look at the red and yellow hollyhocks that were starting to come up, he could see through the open gate into Myrtle's back yard.

Where before there had just been the lawn, now there was a large, above-ground pool with sleek, ribbed flanks. Over the course of the time they had stepped out together, Myrtle had occasionally mentioned her desire to have a swimming pool installed for the grandchildren who sometimes visited her, but she had never done anything about it. Now she had. And recently. There was still some of the packaging on the ground.

Myrtle had had it placed well. The water would be shaded by her honey locust and screened off in the directions that counted by her tall fence. There were two or three other pools like this one in town, but this was far and away the nicest one that Horace had seen. He stood up on his tiptoes and tried to look over the side. He set one of the sodas down on Myrtle's back porch, then took his shoes off and climbed in.

Stepping carefully across the flexible plastic bottom, Horace walked out to the middle and sat down. The walls of the pool were a dusty green. It was a nice color. The honey locust cast its gentle shade and beyond it was the blue Indiana sky. Horace twisted open his soda and took a drink. He gasped, cleared his throat and coughed, leaned the bottle against the side of the pool, and then lay down.

As he watched, first a robin, then a cardinal, then a sparrow flew over the pool. They came in from different directions and at different speeds. When a crow winged over the plastic edge, it started to seem like there was some purpose to it. Like they were trailing gossamer lines. Swimming with Rose-Alice, his war-battered body had been so lean that even the salt-stuffed waters of the Aegean had seemed to want to suck it down. When he had stopped splashing and gone perfectly still, as Rose-Alice had told him he should, only his eyes, nose, and mouth had stayed above water.

Soon, he would need to get back to his mowing, and the other things there surely still were to do, but in the meantime, since no one could see him and it was all right anyway, he spread his arms and legs wide and then arched his spine and tilted back his head.

Horace had said something to Rose-Alice after they had come out of the water—as they had lain beside each other for a few minutes on the smooth warm stones of the beach before going up to meet the truck—something about how most of him hadn't floated, and she had said, "Yes, Mr. Allen, that's true, but some of you did."

Della

Della Dorner's mother, better than half asleep and knuckling at her eyes, said, "On your marks . . ." She said, "Set . . ." She said, "Go!" and yawned and started immediately shuffling back to her bed, but Della, who had shot out of the set of blocks she had placed in the grass next to the top of the driveway, pulled up a few paces later and told her mother it had been a false start.

"False start, my big butt," Della's mother said through another yawn.

"It's not big, Mama. I wobbled. They call that every time," said Della.

"I'm going back to sleep. I was having a good dream."

"Was I in it?"

"I said it was a *good* dream."

"Har, har, har."

Della's mother grinned. She rubbed at her eyes again. She said, "On your marks now, girl. On your marks, let's see what you got." She said, "Set . . ." then stepped forward and swatted Della on the behind, and when she said, "That was 'Go!' goddammit," Della flew down the driveway with a grin on her face.

She ran off strong but smart, like she was going out against Penny Ellingsworth, who had beaten her by an eyelash at Sectionals and Regionals both. She ran and grinned, relaxed in her arms, hands unclenched, long strides, knees high, the way her coach had taught her, "like you care about it!" and almost crashed into old Horace Allen who had stepped into the mouth of her driveway. Della hollered an apology and Horace Allen waved and then got a strange look on his face like his dog had died, but Della kept going, even faster now, full out. It was four hundred meters to the far side of Main. Sometimes she had to adjust her pace because there were cars, but it was early and Main was clear, and after a quick look both ways she went speeding across and only slowed when she was three strides past the finish line: an electric pole next to Ogleby's. She slowed but did not stop. She jogged on another hundred yards and then ducked into a stand of persimmon, horseweed, and creeper vine.

When Della came out the other side, she was on the orange Schwinn five-speed she had hidden in the trees the evening before when she had told her mother she was going over to see how things were coming with the evening shift at the Galaxy Swirl. She rode the Schwinn—a gift from her father whom she had not laid eyes on in sixteen months—straight out Washington into the countryside. It was still cool. The morning air fresh. You could tell it would get hot later, but for now it was perfect. The

world smelled like corn and chicory flower and drying dirt and
woods. Turkey vultures were up riding the currents. Della
pedaled as hard as she had run her four hundred. She considered it training. Everything was training. When she had ridden
for just over a dozen minutes, she got off her bike and laid it
down near the bottom of the drainage ditch where it could not
be seen from the road.

Sugar Henry was waiting for Della in a barn at the north end
of his family's farm. The barn was one of the old round ones you
didn't see many of anymore and a few winters before had had
half its roof fall in. Today it was full of light and dust. Doves
perched in its rafters and sometimes as you went in a pretty
good-sized owl came flapping out. Sugar was sitting on a pile of
empty feed bags with his legs crossed. He looked like he was in
circle back at elementary school, like he was working up his
courage to raise his hand for Show and Tell. Della giggled.
Always happiest when she was sweating, she smeared her
dripping forearm across Sugar's face. He neither moved nor
reacted, and she saw that he had brought with him a pack of
Kraft Singles. Della loved Kraft Singles. They kissed for a while
and then Della pulled away and stuck her hand out.

Generally, the price of a kiss was a slice. A kiss was now understood between them to involve the tongue. When they had first
started, there had been a regular kiss for one slice and a French
kiss for two but now it was all *formidable* and *sacré bleu* and *parlez-
vous français*. There were a number of interesting options for
two slices. Three slices they hadn't quite got there yet. The way
the game worked Sugar brought the Kraft Singles. But they
could both pull from the stack and give it to the other. Another
thing about when it had started was the slice had had to come
first but now it could come after. Sometimes they used Twizzlers

or different kinds of candy. Gum didn't work because part of the game was you had to eat as you went along. Neither of them liked having a giant wad of gum in their mouths while they were getting to it.

They kissed again. They had gotten better at it. The first time they had tried French they had whirled their tongues around like they were eggbeaters. It had been fun but also a little alarming and definitely messy. Once or twice after these initial attempts as Della chewed her Single and felt the wet on her chin she had laughed. Sugar had not laughed. Della thought he looked good when he was being serious. Out in the world with Greg Cullen or any of the others he was full of juice, but in the barn he was different. In the barn with her he was quiet, and she was coming to like it more and more. After they had finished their kiss, and she had unwrapped and eaten her slice, Sugar slid two Singles off the stack and onto the feed bags and Della took off her shirt. They kissed that way for a while and then ate, and then Della slid off two slices of her own and said, "Touch them."

They took a break after that. Sugar had brought them Mountain Dews. His work as a bagger in Frankfort put many such luxuries at his fingertips. Sometimes Della brought drinks from the Galaxy Swirl and once she had come with ice cream sandwiches in a cooler, but mostly it was Sugar who brought the supplies. After he had taken a couple of swigs, he stood up and went over to an old heavy bag hung from a jury-rigged bailing hook. The heavy bag was the reason Sugar gave for coming all the way out to the barn in the morning. As Della watched, he dropped into a crouch and gave it a few zippy lefts. He told her he was working on his jab. After he had punched on the bag a while, he grabbed a jump rope and started whacking the floorboards with it. Dust rose. It was a pleasant kind of dust. Made out of the old ways. This was something Della's grandfather had once said about a song on the radio. Della sometimes wrote his expressions down in her diary. She never said any of them aloud herself, but she often thought about them. Her grandfather had stopped being a sheriff when she was little, but he still had his old cruiser, and every chance she got she went riding in it with him.

Sugar had said from the start that he had to do some working out when they met in the barn so that when he got back to the house he wouldn't have to tell any lies about where he had been. Della understood this. She herself did sometimes lie to her mother about what she had gotten up to when she wasn't home, but she preferred to have the cover of a run she had at least in some way undertaken. After a while Sugar set the jump rope aside and did forty pushups. He was soon sweating as much as Della had been when she arrived. Once for fun she had sat down on his back while he was in the middle of a set of twenty. He had kept going like she wasn't there and he hadn't said anything about it when just before he finished she had jumped up and off and fallen laughing onto the feed bags. At work the following afternoon she had asked Greg how many pushups he could do. He had said a number and she had asked him how many he could do with 120 pounds on his back. Greg had understood what the 120 pounds had referred to and blushed. He blushed a lot. Della suspected Greg couldn't do a single pushup with her sitting on him, much less nine or ten. When Greg had gone out to the shed that day to get more soft-serve cones, Della dropped to the floor of the Freeze and managed five pushups. Later, when they were closing, Della had dropped again and asked Greg to put one of the twenty-pound boxes of chocolate sprinkles on her, but he had blushed again and told her to fuck off.

Sugar had a pretty sheen to him when he came back over to
the feed bags. Before he sat down, he pulled a strip of cloth out
of the crumpled Marsh bag he'd brought their supplies in and
wiped at his face with it. Then he tied it around his forehead so
that he wouldn't, presumably, drip too much during the next
round. Della wanted to tell him to take it off, to tell him that it
looked too silly. But she liked it. It was stupid but it looked good.
"There is an elegance to the world you can't always account for"
was something else her grandfather said. Della had put two thick
lines under it in her journal and thought about it when she qual-
ified for Sectionals and someone complimented her on how
handsomely she had run. She had been on JV all season but then,
during an invitational meet at Delphi, she had raced everyone
off the track. She was going for State next year. "Work your tail
off you might actually get there," her grandfather had said.

When Sugar sat back down, she told him to cross his legs
again show-and-tell style like he'd had them at the start and
then, moving very slowly, like she'd seen it done in a movie, she
straddled him. Looking him in his practically unblinking eyes,
she grabbed the bottom of his T-shirt and yanked it up and over
his head. Both of them flicked their eyes over to the stack of
Kraft Singles after she had tossed the T-shirt aside. There
weren't that many slices left. Della reached over and slid off
three. Sugar cocked his head to one side, curious. Della glanced
down at the front of her bra then back up at him.

"Unhook it," she said.

When both Sugar's sweat-shiny arms rose up off the floor to
accomplish the task, she intercepted one of them. She pressed
it back down to the floor. She snugged herself up a little closer
to him. She liked the way this made him gasp a little.

"Be suave," she said.

Della didn't get a chance to learn if Sugar was up to the task of one-handed bra unhooking or how he would react once he had either succeeded or she had helped him—and they had taken things fully into mysterious three-slice territory—because just as his fingers had started to flutter, there arrived in their ears the sound of an engine. And that engine was Sugar's father's backhoe coming along the lane. This was not the first time it or something like it had happened while they were at their play.

"He'll be wanting to hit on the bag with me," Sugar said.

"Well then," said Della, picking up one of the Singles and unwrapping it and shoving all of it in Sugar's mouth, then taking the other two and unwrapping them and shoving them in hers so that her next words, "I better go," came out garbled.

Pulling her T-shirt on as she went, Della ran straight out through what had once been the west wall of the barn. She had a whole beanfield to get across. If she ran just fast enough, Mr. Henry wouldn't see her before she had crossed it. She felt pleased as she ran because (1) it was exciting to have gotten out just before getting caught and (2) because the approach of Mr. Henry had meant there didn't have to be any drawn-out farewells. Sugar was funny about saying goodbye. He was more or less a nice-looking log of wood through most of their games, but when it was time to get going he turned sentimental, mushy almost, and everything started taking twice as long. Even just now as she was getting ready to run, with the backhoe drawing closer by the second, Sugar had grabbed her hand and held it like she was going away to college and hadn't yet made him any promise.

As she ran, Della tried to picture what Sugar's face would have looked like had they made it all the way through to three-slice country, but she couldn't quite get there. She wondered what she would have looked like when she was looking at him looking at her. Would he have noticed her doing this? She didn't think so. Just like she didn't think they were going to start officially dating. God that would be weird. But did weird mean it wouldn't happen? Taking a crap was weird, but you did it every day. Well, when you weren't constipated. "Nothing is nothing, Della," her grandfather had said several times as they were driving around. He had often told her about the loves he had attempted to cultivate after her grandmother had died. Each love had been very different.

His fondest of these loves, even though it had gone ultimately unrequited, was Zorrie Underwood. Della knew Zorrie a little. Every now and again she came into the Galaxy Swirl for a softserve. She always looked to Della like she'd just leaned back out of a grain bin or climbed down off a tractor. She was nice. But not too nice. Della wished it had worked out. What did she wish about Sugar? About her life? She started to say "I wish . . ." but it got turned into "Ah shit . . ." before it could get all the way out. For when she emerged from the field and the soybean leaves were no longer slapping at her legs, she could not only hear the sound of the backhoe engine growing louder like she wasn't now 275 yards from the barn but still sitting inside it kissing on Sugar Henry, she also saw that her bike was gone.

Della knew she had two choices: jump back into the beans and hide or run. Run like that was the all and everything of what she was out here doing on a gravel road two and a half miles from town. Something told her run. And this was the right instinct because before she would have made it back into the beans, Sugar's father's bright blue backhoe came juddering and bouncing off the lane and onto the road. Della assumed what she thought was the posture of a girl who had been out for the exercise she was supposed to have been getting. And when the backhoe came up behind and then beside her, she thought she'd squared the circle just fine. Only when she turned to wave casually at Mr. Henry like wasn't it a wonderful morning out here in God's country to be either out running or working a backhoe, she saw that it was actually Sugar's mother driving and also that her missing Schwinn, looking like a dead orange deer, was in the pelican pouch of the front shovel. Mrs. Henry did not turn to look at Della, only overtook her and went ahead fast down the road. When she got to the Henry property line—part of an old concrete post with some cast-iron gate still attached to it—she stopped the machine and tipped the shovel and dropped the bike out onto the gravel. She then executed a tight turn, almost a 180, and started back in Della's direction. When they drew even with each other, Mrs. Henry barked out that she would be placing a phone call right damn smart to Della's mother, and Della said, "All right only could you wait a little while because she got in late and she's probably still sleeping," and Mrs. Henry gave out a humorless guffaw over her shoulder and shouted, "Your goose is cooked, hon!"

Della rode all the way home. Her heart was beating hard and her mouth tasted like cheese. She wished she had taken another swig of Mountain Dew. Not that she minded the taste of cheese. Or whatever it was. Her grandfather usually kept some in his fridge for her, but he had more than once read out the list of ingredients and had her make her own sandwiches with it. This didn't keep the stack from getting shorter between her visits. When she made this observation, he either winked and said, "Don't sass me, Della Dorner," or winked and said, "The mice around here must sure like fake cheese." Della considered, for a moment, riding out right then to see her grandfather, but he lived six miles in the wrong direction and showing up would have taken too much explaining. Her mother didn't like complicated stories. She often evoked the "K.I.S.S." principle: "keep it simple, stupid." Della did her best to live by those four words.

Her mother, an ER nurse pulling too many doubles this month, really would almost definitely still be asleep and wouldn't see her when she pedaled rather than ran back up the driveway, so there wasn't any need to re-hide her bike and make like she was trotting back into the stable after a long run. Della's mother had an awe-inspiring capacity for fathomless sleep once she got going. Della had caught her earlier on a trip to the bathroom and had begged her hard enough that she had complied to come out and serve as race official. She hadn't been kidding, though, about getting back to her dreams.

When Della got home, she peeked in on her mother. There she was, lying on her back, ever so lightly snoring. Della thought that her mother was very beautiful when she was sleeping. That she looked noble, like someone in a painting, maybe of Queen Elizabeth the First or Joan of Arc. She did not look like someone who was waiting for a prince to come and kiss her. It wasn't a Sleeping Beauty thing. Della's mother was tough. She was the one the doctors wanted to be there at the end of a long shift. She was the one whose door you knocked on when the corn chips were down. When she was younger, Della had made her mother the star of numerous fantasies to do with conquest and endurance. Often her mother had been cast in the role of champion to an ailing king. The ailing king would be on the brink of defeat, and Della's mother would step forward, smiling grimly, with a deadly saber in her hand. Sometimes Della had served as her mother's page in these fantasies. The two of them had ridden out together in search of adventure that would bring glory to the kingdom and, you know why not, considerable personal reward.

After pouring herself a glass of water and drinking it all the way down, Della took a quick shower because she had sweat so much and had work later. While she was titrating the water down from lukewarm to cool, the phone rang. It rang again a few minutes later while she was drying off. When it rang a third time, after she had got dressed and had had another drink, she cleared her throat and picked up. She had always been good at imitating her mother's voice, and there was no question that she nailed the initial, "This is she . . ." Indeed, Mrs. Henry got right to the point. Della had been whoring with Sugar in the old barn on their property, and she was going to end up knocked up. That wouldn't be good for Della and it wouldn't be good for Sugar or for any of them.

"No, it wouldn't, Tammy," Della agreed.

Della, employing one of her mother's tics, used Mrs. Henry's first name numerous times during what followed. She said that while as a Christian she didn't like to hear words like *whoring* and *knocked up* she could understand why she, Tammy, had gotten upset enough to employ them. She had been there herself many a time. Lord, yes, she had. She said it must have been a shock to poor Tammy to find out what was going on. She had her hands full with Della. You never knew what that crazy girl would get up to next.

"Why, Tammy, sometimes I get to thinking that next thing you know it she'll be kidnapping babies!"

"Kidnapping babies!" Mrs. Henry said. She agreed that it must be hard for her, Della's mother, to raise up a girl like that. She said she didn't begrudge the kids some fun and they'd all been young once, but too much was too much and after a while it got to be plain old ass-tanning time.

"Amen, Tammy," Della said. "Tammy, Amen."

Not sure how long she could keep it up, Della started clearing her throat and saying "Well . . ." the way her mother did when she was done being on the phone, but then there was some noise in the background, maybe Mr. Henry, and Mrs. Henry said, "I got someone here has something he wants to say to you." Before Della could protest, the phone changed hands and Della's partner in crime came on.

"I'm very sorry," Sugar said.

"Say, 'ma'am,' when you're saying your piece," Mrs. Henry said.

"I'm very sorry, ma'am," said Sugar.

"That's all right," Della said.

Mrs. Henry and maybe Mr. Henry, too, whispered something then, and Sugar cleared his throat and went on.

"What I did was wrong. I was taking advantage. I should have known better. It was disrespectful to Della and to you."

After some additional prompting from Mrs. Henry, Sugar then discoursed, at some length, about trying to be a good student and a Christian, as well as an athlete in his way. While he spoke, Della tried to imagine the look on his face. On the one hand, it sounded like he was reading from a script, and on the other, he couldn't have been. What look did he get when he was being unlike himself? At least as she understood him. Maybe this was his real self. Or one of them. There was the Sugar from the barn when he was with her and the Sugar when he was with his friends and now there was the in-trouble Sugar talking into a phone. Were there other Sugars? Other Dellas? How many of them were there?

And what was it about his expressions that got to her? Was it that he had any expressions to offer at all? Was she primed to wish for the void to smile at her? Della's father had not said goodbye when he left. He had just drifted away. Like a smoke curl. She had four pictures of him and he looked the same in each one. Big teeth under a little moustache. Della's mother said he'd be back. That they just had to give him time. "Time is just a figure of speech," her grandfather had said. He had never much liked her father. Or liked him at all. But he had never been unfair or unkind, and when Della's mother had said one Sunday afternoon in the middle of a big bite of thick-slice ham that he was gone and Della's grandfather had said, "Well then I'll go get him," and Della's mother had said, "No. You. Will. Not," Della's grandfather had said, "All right, Bethie," and he had kept his word. Della wondered how Sugar was with keeping promises. How could you know? Sugar never let on what he was really thinking when he was with her. Even now she couldn't be sure what she was hearing had anything to do with what he really thought.

He ought to be a politician. Maybe that's what he was. Her father made long speeches on the phone sometimes too, but that was when he'd been drinking. He wasn't a mean drunk. He just got talkative and stupid. Della wished Sugar had taken her bra off. Now that would have been something. She wondered if he had or if she had gone ahead and done it for him if he would have been struck entirely dumb. If he would still be sitting there even now, even as he was making his speech on the phone to her mother, sitting there with his hands slack at his sides and his eyes fixing to pop out.

Della got so wrapped up in thinking that she forgot what she was doing and who she was supposed to be and started, without realizing she was doing it, with the image of dumb-struck Sugar floating before her, to laugh. When Sugar, mumbling at that moment about trust and faith, stopped, confused, Della quit laughing and asked him what he would be willing to do if she handed him four Kraft Singles or, hell, the whole damn stack, right there, right that second, and then she said, "Think about it, Sugar Henry. And come see me later at work. And for now just say, 'I understand.' Say, 'I will do that.' Say, 'you can count on me.' Say 'yes, ma'am.'"

After she had hung up the phone, Della went and stood in the doorway of her mother's room. "I think Sugar Henry and I are dating," she announced. There was no response. When she was small, she had gone through a period of worrying that her mother was dead when she would sleep on and on like this. Her father had always been nice about it. He had told her to take her mother's hand and tell him whether it was warm or cold, and she had done so and said "warm." He had then told her to put her ear on her mother's back and tell him what she heard, and she had said "her heart." If Della's fear still hadn't passed, he would then tell her to put her cheek near her mother's mouth and tell him what she felt. She did this now. Her mother was on her side with her mouth slightly open. Della lay down. She scooted quietly over so her face was close to her mother's.

"What do you feel?" her father asked.

"Her breath," Della said.

"Blessed breath," her father said.

And that was just right.

Toby

When Toby Slocum's much-prized Casio FX-82 started beeping at 3 P.M., his mind carefully folded up his "Honk If You Love the Gipper!!!" sign and shoved it in his father's old ROTC duffel and went running off ahead of him to the Galaxy Swirl. There it ordered his usual vanilla cone with cosmic sprinkles and three napkins and started working its tongue over the pebbly sweet softness as it walked off along Main and cut west to head home. Toby was surprised, then, to discover that the Galaxy Swirl was actually still closed. This was just strange enough—he could not remember it ever having happened in the six years since it had opened—that after Toby had peered in the windows and seen the soft-serve and soda and Slushee machines illuminated, he went around back past the empty side tables to see if Della Dorner and Greg Cullen might be doing something crazy like taking a break. The back door stood open. Toby called out. As soon as he did, he heard Greg's voice coming from the shed. Greg's voice asked him to please get the key hanging on a hook next to the cup dispenser and let him "the fuck" out. Toby got the key. Behind the counter, where he had never been, the shop smelled strongly of bleach and vanilla. The machines seemed much louder up close than they did from where you ordered. The floor was shiny. There was a pile of aprons in one corner and a Pioneer seed company calendar on the wall. Toby put his hand on the side of the cash register. It was warm to the touch. He was pretty sure he knew which button would open it, but of course he didn't press it. It bothered him too much to imagine someone might think he was there to steal. The shed door was easy to unlock. Greg burst out with his shirt in his hand. Toby asked him why he had his shirt off and why the Galaxy Swirl wasn't open.

"I came for my cone," Toby explained.

Greg didn't answer. Instead, he hung his shirt over his arm, took a deep breath, put his hands together like it was Sunday and time to say a prayer, and then bowed. After he had straightened back up, he grunted and ran off.

Toby poked his head inside the shed. He didn't think anyone would find any fault with that. He saw three empty Dr Pepper cans and a half-empty bag of sour cream and onion chips. The shed didn't smell good. There was a hole in the side of one of the big bags of flour. Toby went back over to the Galaxy Swirl. This time he noticed an Igloo cooler sitting next to the back door. He also saw that a piece of green cloth was draped across the top of the cash register. A red light on the phone that sat in the little alcove next to the counter was beeping. The alcove was a mess. Toby picked up a cone and filled it with vanilla ice cream. He did not mean to take too much, but he had never used the machine before and some spilled off the cone and onto the back of his thumb. He had seen this happen twice to Greg and once to Della, so he didn't feel bad about it. Della had said "well, shit!" when it happened, then had licked it off and laughed. Greg had said nothing and had not licked off the extra ice cream. Each time Greg had set the cone down and wiped his hand carefully with a wet cloth. Toby liked Della better than he liked Greg, so he did what Della had done. He even laughed as she had, though he did not say "shit." Toby did not go in for cuss words. His mother had liked them a great deal. His father had liked them even more. Toby dipped his cone in the glittery cosmic sprinkles, deposited one dollar on the counter and dropped a quarter in the tip jar, took three napkins, and left.

He set his stopwatch when he stepped onto Main. Since acquiring his Casio at the K-Mart in Frankfort, he had begun cultivating an interest in the detailed passage of time. It took him, on average, twenty-three minutes and fifteen seconds to walk home. From the time he started to the McDermott ditch on W Washington—ten minutes and twenty seconds—he did what he always did, which was to eat the ice cream and sprinkle mixture as slowly as he could without it turning entirely into soup while thinking, simultaneously, about the Gipper. He thought about the Gipper's acting career and about the Gipper's wife and children and about the Gipper's time as governor of California and about the Gipper's great victory in the 1980 presidential race. He thought about how the Gipper had defeated Jimmy Carter. He thought about the gleam in the Gipper's eye when he smiled. He thought about the Gipper's fine voice. He imagined the Gipper walking alongside him and finishing off his own ice cream and telling Toby that it had been just as good an ice cream as Toby had said it would be and that that made Toby a real square guy. The Gipper put his hand on Toby's shoulder

when he said this. He winked at Toby. He looked Toby in the
eye and said, "Toby, my friend, everything is going to be just
grand."

Toby licked at his cone and thought about holding up his
Gipper sign and about people honking their approval. Sometimes people gave Toby the old thumbs up after honking. Toby
liked getting the old thumbs up. It was of course something that
the Gipper did frequently. For a long time, Toby had held up a
"Honk If You Love Jesus!!!" sign on Main and had sometimes
also walked along the back roads around Bright Creek with it,
but though he had received the old thumbs up for Jesus, it had
never seemed to him like something Jesus himself would do.
Jesus and the Gipper had many things in common but diverged,
in Toby's opinion, when it came to hand gestures.

Toby didn't have to think about the Gipper anymore once he
was past the McDermott Ditch. He could think about anything
he wanted. That was his rule. Toby liked to have rules. For a long
time, they had been mostly set for him and now he set them for
himself. He was hoping that knowing how long things took
rather than how far he had gone or how long things took *and*
how far he had gotten while he was doing them would help him
make better rules and improve his life. He didn't yet know how
the fact that his mind was so often running off away from him
would fit into this. He didn't know how time worked in his mind.
Maybe it was the same. But he doubted it. Usually it was about
now, after the ten minutes and twenty seconds of walking that
had taken him to the McDermott Ditch, that he and his mind
joined back up. He and his mind had both eaten their ice cream
down to the cone by this time. They were both holding the cone
carefully in their hand. In this way he and his mind were very
similar. In other ways, like Jesus and the Gipper, they were not.

For example, when Toby started singing, he knew for sure that he and his mind had rejoined forces: Toby's mind, not Toby, knew all the songs.

The first thing Toby did when he got home was throw his father's ROTC sack up on the porch, and the second thing he did, after restarting his stopwatch, was head out back to feed the cone he had saved to his donkey, Miss Mack. Miss Mack loved a sugary ice cream cone. Toby thought the cones looked good up against her nutmeg-color coat. The piece of green cloth that had been draped over the cash register at the Galaxy Swirl would also have looked good against her coat. In general, it suited her to be surrounded by green, though different shades of purple weren't bad for her either. Toby was still singing. He hadn't really stopped. He didn't know how she felt about it, but he had decided a while ago that he should always be singing when he went to see Miss Mack. Every once in a while, he didn't catch up with his mind until they were both walking the narrow path behind the house out to the barn, which made this difficult. But usually, like today, it was all right. Toby had a good repertory of popular and show tunes. He could even sing some of the new ones. Today he was singing "Don't You Want Me" by the Human League. The path had nice acoustics for singing. Toby's father had once said this. It had nice acoustics because it was lined with the washers and driers and ovens and refrigerators (which lay on their sides) that Toby's father had during the years before his death been planning to refurbish to sell in a store he was never quite able to take possession of. When this plan had not come to fruition, his thoughts, not for the first time in those later years, had taken a creative turn.

The path was the central alley in a grand design—part grail and part trident—that Toby's father, inspired by carefully studied

photographs of hillside chalk drawings in England, had elaborated in the open acre between the house and the barn. The
design had changed several times before it was implemented.
Toby had often sat with his father in the evening as he drew
sketches. When the grail/chalice schema had been settled on
and elaborated to his satisfaction, which had required several
rounds of rearrangement, Toby's father had paid an aerial
photographer out of Kokomo to show them "what the heavens
saw." In the event what the heavens saw was somewhat too
obscured by pignut hickory to be parsed. Given the imperfect
result, Toby's father had had the image framed and set above
the mantle, but had let go of making photocopies to distribute
to everyone at church. After they had stopped shifting things
around, first the surrounding lawn and then the horseweed and
then the daylilies had come for the design. As if moved to offer
an additional example of the appetite of nature, Toby's mother
had over her own last years, which had stretched beyond Toby's
father's, planted a huge number of perennials in and around the
straight and curving rows, even setting some highly successful
honeysuckle loose on it before she passed. Now the whole was
home to rabbits, possums, chipmunks, mice, bees, butterflies,
and an impressive number of gorgeous, grouchy humming-
birds. Only the central alley, which led to the barn, was still easily
navigable. Toby's father had called this alley the "heart of the
grail" or the "central spike of the trident," depending on his
mood. Toby's mother had called it the "way I get to my barn."

In the early part of their marriage, Toby's mother had been
the one with all the personality. After high school, and before
meeting Toby's father, she had lived for a year in West Lafayette,
where she had attended lectures at Purdue on art history and
literature. Her books were still in the library on the second floor.

Seven notebooks filled with her "youthful scribblings" still sat on the shelves. There would have been twice as many more except that she had made a fire of the more imaginative ones before she would consent to climb into the marriage bed. The resultant plume of smoke and cinder had inspired her, as she later explained it to Toby, to build up a series of black and red floral arrangements all around her new husband's property, a move that some of the neighbors found alarming. Then, after Toby's birth there had been a painting phase. After some while of this Toby's father encouraged a music teacher from the high school in town, whose furnace he had repaired, and who seemed to know something about the fine as well as the musical arts, to come out for a visit. There were pigs, sheep, and chickens living in the barn where Toby's mother had her studio, and the prospect was both too noisy and too fragrant for the music teacher, who quickly retreated to her Ford. Fortunately, she had brought along the new French teacher, a Miss Ray, who they learned had traveled as far away in the world as Europe. Miss Ray spoke favorably about both theme and composition in Toby's mother's work. She talked about the interesting choice of color in some of the larger canvases and remarked on the precision of hand on display in a series of studies of fishing lures. During the entirety of the visit, Toby, then five or six, and the artist herself crouched hidden and quietly giggling behind the stack of hay bales she had rigged into a makeshift easel. Toby's mother kept pretending she was going to pull the top bale and the painting-in-progress young Miss Ray had taken a particular interest in—a study of grain bins—down on top of them.

Something she managed to resist doing even after they poked their heads out from behind the bales to watch the polite young teacher go over to the window, reach into her handbag, extract a firecracker and a box of matches, light the fuse, blow out the match, and toss the burning thing out the window. In the wake of the impressive explosion, Miss Ray turned, smiled, and said to Toby, who had not pulled his head back quickly enough, "Tell your mother that's how much I like her paintings." Toby and his father clapped after Miss Ray and the music teacher had driven away, and Toby's mother bowed and curtseyed both, and they all kept saying "Boom!" right up until bedtime, but the next morning all the paintings, including the one of a rocket riding the Milky Way that she had hung in Toby's bedroom, were, over Toby's father's protests, tossed onto the burning pile and doused with fuel oil.

A period of buying colorful old dresses from garage and estate sales as far away as Indianapolis and Muncie had followed. Toby's mother never said what she planned to do with all these dresses, and most of them still hung in the attic. It was during the period that the dresses were being accumulated that Toby's father caught the bug and began making pencil sketches and checking picture books out of the library. For a few weeks he amused himself by welding pieces of metal together in unlikely configurations. Then he tried his hand at whittling, which saw mixed results, followed by a fairly successful stab at making sculpture with his chainsaw. Toby's mother took the stance of an amused onlooker. There seemed to be an understanding between them that she was not to be consulted, that the artistic floor was his now, that she had gotten out of the game. Once, Toby heard her on the phone describing one of her father's efforts as "just awful," but she said it in such an affectionate tone that it made Toby think afterward that maybe what she had said was "just wonderful."

Wonderful was unquestionably the word she used to describe how she felt after she took up regular exercising. At first she contented herself with the daily regimen of calisthenics prescribed for her after a resurgence of childhood rheumatic fever had kept her bedridden for close to a month. Toby had done some of these exercises with her, and even when she added vigorous squats and chin-ups, as well as several techniques adapted from the Charles Atlas dynamic tension scheme, he continued. The subsequent twice-daily weight-lifting sessions on the paint-spattered floor of her former studio was too much for him though. Toby sometimes went to sit with a comic book just outside the room and listen to the grunting and clanking. She and his father took to weekly arm-wrestling matches, and sometimes Toby would place his hand on his mother's bicep as time and again she proved to his father the success of her method.

Despite the example of his parents, Toby managed to get through childhood unifected by any particular artistic or athletic inclinations. Though he was never "the brightest bulb in the box," he was generally well-enough liked at school and was a whiz with anything to do with animals. It was in caring for an ailing ewe, one he couldn't leave alone even for a few minutes, that he had first discovered how easy it was for his mind to wander off. One time it wandered up into the attic and put on one of his mother's dresses. When late that night the ewe was out of danger, he followed after it and did the same. He and his mind went to the attic frequently after that, both separately and together. Once his mother climbed up while he was putting on one of her dresses. When he turned, she looked him wonderingly in the eye and gently put a hand on his cheek.

She was not nearly so understanding about how hard and fast
he later fell for Jesus. After he made his first sign and went out
to walk around in town for a few hours and she saw him standing
by the bank with it, she picked up the family Bible when he got
home and banged herself on the head. He didn't know how to
tell her what Jesus did for him. That he provided a kind of outlet
for feelings he didn't know how to put into words. He didn't go
out again with his sign until she, like his father before her, had
passed. He sometimes wondered now how she would feel about
his Gipper sign. Toby's mind had several times dashed off into
death and asked her about it, but though it found her easily
enough, she never chose to respond. His mind always came
across her sitting by a fire and surrounded by the instruments
of her earthly preoccupations: barbells and paintbrushes and
flower petals. Other objects, like a harp and a sextant, he could
not make sense of. His father was never around.

Miss Mack was not in her stall. This was not terribly unusual.
About once every two weeks she absented herself, and Toby, who
never latched that door to her stall, thought of this as a small
price to pay for her contentment. There were neighbors, though,
who didn't think much of a wandering donkey, and lately Miss
Mack had taken to leaving the property entirely, either ambling
down to the creek for a drink and nibble or over to the old
schoolyard, where her favored thistles grew up around the derelict building in profusion. His mind went running off down the
creek path. His mind crossed the creek and spotted Miss Mack
nibbling lily leaves on the Randall property. His mind whispered
into her ear as it scratched the top of her skull and then held out
the sticky, softened cone. She gave it an interested nibble, and
so Toby understood he should keep the sticky thing a little
longer. Unfortunately, when cone in hand he had crossed the

creek and left behind the property his parents had willed him after first selling off half of it so that the proceeds could sustain him, and made it to the daylilies that marked an old corn crib he had once long ago now taken a nap in—until Mr. Randall, its owner, had yelled at him for loitering and yelled so long it made him cry until he threw up, so that when they found out both his parents had gone tearing off to the Randalls with him in tow and had beaten on the door until Mr. Randall came out with a twelve-gauge and both of Toby's parents pointed at their chests and said only very slightly different versions of "You better shoot us, you motherfucker, because if you ever holler at our boy again we will come back with dynamite and we will put it under your porch and we will blow the front of your fucking house off!"—he found his mind but not his donkey.

Toby's mind, though, had something interesting to say as it slipped softly back into his skull. It told him to look at the wall of corn standing just beyond the daylilies that his donkey had not, as it turned out, interested herself in. His mind told him to look closely. He knew immediately who it was standing three, not four, rows in.

"Hi Gladys," he said. Not everyone knew that Gladys Bacon liked to go for walks in the fields. She would walk from field to field, never leaving the corn except when there was some shadow laid down as a bridge. It didn't matter what kind of shadow it was. She never took her walks on cloudy days. Nor did she carry an umbrella. Those were her rules. She had told Toby, who had chanced on her one day stepping out of the stalks by the bridge, that the walks were a kind of puzzle for her, a way to test her memory and her smarts as she traveled from point A to point B. Given the vicissitudes of crop rotation and growing speeds, the puzzle wasn't anywhere near as simple as it seemed. Gladys now pushed through the emerald rows, making the tassels slide open and quiver shut just above her. Without leaving the field, she peered out at him through the final row. It looked to Toby like she was dressed for a party. She had on a bright yellow skirt and a blue blouse. There was sweat showing around her armpits. She was wearing a sun visor and dangling a pair of heels from her left hand.

"Hello, Toby Slocum," she said.

Gladys had small gray eyes and a beautiful big nose. She had on perfume. Generally, Toby didn't like perfume, but this one, when it reached him, reminded him a little of the verbena tea his mother had favored at the end of her life.

"The Galaxy Swirl was closed this afternoon," he said.

"Was it?"

"It was."

"Then where'd you get that cone?"

Toby looked at the sorry thing he was holding and blushed. He said, "My donkey's gone on one of her walks."

"Like me I reckon . . ."

"Oh, Miss Mack would never step into a cornfield."

"And I'd just about as soon never step out of one."

"But it's kind of the same."

"Yes, it kind of is."

"How's Wendell coming?"

"Oh, he's good."

Toby knew that Wendell, who had fought over in Vietnam, probably wasn't really coming all that well, but Toby gave Gladys the old thumbs-up anyway. She stuck her free fist out between two corn stalks and gave him the old thumbs-up right back. The way she hooked her arm out and around the stalks created the illusion that it was the corn that was making the gesture, like she was part of the field. Gladys always honked when she passed Toby holding his Gipper sign. She had honked at least three or four times over the years for Jesus too. Toby wondered what Gladys would make of the differences between them. He didn't ask her though, and after a few seconds she pulled her fist back into the field.

"There's more starlings than usual out and about," she said.

"Starlings?"

"Doesn't matter. And anyways I need to get going. Shadow from yonder mulberry is about to lay itself flat all the way over into Gale Evans's front forty."

"Do you want to borrow my watch? It's really nice. You could time things and know what time it is as you go and it tells the date."

"I know what time it is, honey. It's time for that mulberry to throw its shadow."

"Are you heading over to visit with your folks?"

Gladys nodded. "Catch them up on things. It's been a while. I left my car at Candy Wilson's. Myrtle Kelly's got the keys. She'll come and fetch me after a while."

Toby watched Gladys fade back into the corn, then he recrossed the creek and went home in case Miss Mack had got bored and come back. She had not. Before he followed his mind over to the old school, to see if it had gotten things right this time, which it probably had, he went inside and pulled a bottle of milk out of the fridge and then stood there on the warm blue linoleum his parents had once spent a full month of evenings trying to agree on and drank almost three quarters of it straight down. Toby had been a fiend for drinking cold milk straight out of the bottle since he was small. Whenever his mother had caught him at it, she had either smacked his palm with a wooden

spoon or spanked him or pinched on his ear, though none of it
was ever too hard. Sometimes, when his mother was out running
errands or clanking her weights, Toby's father called him into
the kitchen and the two of them took turns at taking long, cold
drinks. One of the last things Toby could remember his mother
telling him was that soon he could drink all the damn milk
straight out of the bottle that he liked. She had often said "damn."
Damn seemed all right. It wasn't like most of the other things
she and his father had liked to say. Toby put the milk back in the
fridge and wiped at his mouth with the top of his wrist and said,
"That milk was damn delicious." He then wiped his wrist on the
back of his shirt. He thought about setting what was left of the
cone down on the counter and getting it when he came back, but
since his mind was still holding the sorry-looking thing as it
approached Miss Mack by the schoolyard thistles, it went with
him when he walked out the door.

Toby started his stopwatch when he stepped off the front
porch. He walked quickly, like his mind had done, because it
was worried that the wrong person might spot Miss Mack.
There were plenty of people in town who would see an old
donkey working even just a thistle patch and make a fuss. Indeed,
as Toby walked, his mind was seeing people approach the
schoolyard. They looked angry. One of them called out, "Go
on, get out of here!" and brandished a broom. Only it wasn't
Miss Mack she was fussing at in his mind. Miss Mack wasn't
even there. The woman was calling up into the trees. The oaks
and hickories and maples and sycamores were full of starlings. And suddenly the air was full of calls and the ground was
covered in mess. After a while, as if they had been summoned,
boys came forward. Proudly, carefully holding Daisy BB guns.
Toby's mind could see Ben Jeffers, Stephen Hunt, Champ

Cullen, Tommy Whitworth, and others whose names he couldn't recall. All of them were older than him and allowed to have a gun. As the adults watched, the boys began shaking BBs into the chambers, ratcheting their weapons, removing their safeties, aiming and then firing with small, snapping pops. The adults laughed and coached and called out hits as birds began to fall. After a time of it the adults went back to their business, but the boys stayed on. Dropping bird after bird. Calling out encouragement to one another. Making a count.

First Toby's father and then Toby's mother came up beside his mind as it watched, and told it, placing gentle hands on its back, that it didn't have to look, that it didn't have to watch things hurt and die and could leave anytime. But Toby's mind didn't want to leave, it wanted to stay, more than anything in the world, and they allowed it to. And so struck was Toby by the terrible beauty of this permission his mind had been given, which seemed to go well beyond watching boys kill birds, that when he himself arrived at the actual schoolyard and Miss Mack came over from the actual thistle patch and bumped him with her head, and then bumped him again and began licking and nibbling at the forgotten cone, it took him a while, which his watch wasn't going to help measure, to realize that even though he had been the one doing the looking, it was she who had found him.

Lois

Today we had club, but before that I went to the dump.
There was a lot to haul. Half the load was cardboard
from Myrtle's new pool. I was as happy to have it as she was to
be shut of it so that worked out pretty well. I cut myself a pretty
good one stuffing it all in the back of the Kingswood though.
When Alma saw my finger at club and I told her what had
happened, she said I ought to have put a match to my cardboard like any ordinary Dumbo would. I told her I guess that
makes me an extraordinary Dumbo. We call each other
different kinds of Dumbos quite a bit. I told her that it was too
much to burn and that I had so much because I was helping
Myrtle, and she raised up her eyebrows and kind of pursed her
lips. What I didn't tell her because I don't tell her everything
was that Horst Richards who runs the dump likes to see

cardboard in a load. That he likes to spread it out on the approach. Horst says it provides cushion and traction both. It is certainly nice and springy under the wheels when you leave the gravel lane and start climbing the trash hill.

Horst is always waiting up top. I've never not seen him there since he took it over. His daddy was gone half the time. I didn't like his daddy. He was just like the rest of them. But Horst is nice. He'll wink at you. He winks at me every time he sees the big bag of cardboard I bring him. And sometimes he gives me a bow. He didn't bow today but sometimes he does. He only charges me a few dollars when it ought to be more. His father charged me twice or three times as much for next to nothing. Really just the smallest loads. Talk about a real Dumbo. Horst says he won't rob a lady. I believe him. Alma laughed when I told her I must be an extraordinary Dumbo. She had on a dress that showed her fat knees, and she smelled like a candle shop. I wore my red visor. Candy had on some cute purple sunglasses. I asked her where she got them, and she said they'd had them on special at K-Mart, which means tomorrow I may run into town. I won't be doing any more running tonight though. Only place I'll be running is up to bed once I'm done setting this down. I like setting things down. I didn't think I would but I do. This is only my fourth time of doing it, but I can tell I'll keep it up. It can be my hobby. I haven't had one in a while. You can't just watch TV all the time. Horst had on that green shirt I like. He is letting his mustache grow. He has the kind of face a mustache favors. Which is not every face on this poor old planet. I do not say that it is a handsome face. Just that a mustache looks good on it.

Alma and I got into it a little bit. We'd already talked about the cardboard and then we were at the snack table, and she took a look at my plate and whistled and said I'd better take it easy

on the tacos if I wanted to keep impressing my fancy man. I said
"what fancy man, Alma?" and she said "Horst Richards, Dumbo."
Even though it was just the two of us at the table right then, she
said it louder than she should have and I'm pretty sure Laetitia
heard. So I let her have it with both barrels. I told her if anyone
needed to take it easy on the tacos it was her. I said if she didn't
watch it, pretty soon she'd have the whole henhouse et up and
half the hog shed too. She had a mouthful of sunshine salad
when I said this and you could see she was fixing to come back
at me with a good one, but then Candy called out that it was time
for the second round. Myrtle was the lucky one for most of
the day. For about the first half of it I might as well not even have
unsacked my marbles, but that changed on the last couple of
rounds. Those rounds are the doubles and triples. Jeepers, that
was fun. I love to hear the clatter of the marbles. There is nothing
sweeter than when they land just where you want them to. I went
all in on the doubles and had a pile I put down on the final triple.
We have our own rules for Razzle Dazzle. It isn't like the way
they play it down in Cuba and Texas. Where the whole point is
to fleece the foolish. We took a lot of breaks as usual. Laetitia
kept singing the whole time, which was annoying especially since
we took a vote last meeting that singing was bad for concentration and should be limited even if the whole thing is just tossing
marbles in a box. There's still some skill to it. We all think so.
We'd already had a vote about laughing when a game is going
on. That was to keep Myrtle under control. Myrtle could laugh
the roof right off a house. Before we made the rule you'd be
getting ready to make your play at craps or penny poker or
euchre or something but giving it one more thought and then
there'd come the laugh. It's not like she talks loud. I've known

her for seventy years. It's been the same since grade school. Still, I heard her laughing only once today. She must really be working at it. Anyone can change. She was out on the porch with Gladys Bacon when she laughed that one time. I don't know what they were talking about. Gladys came back inside first.

This was a better meeting than last time. Birdie Barnes keeps a clean house, but all she sets out are chips and dips. Chips and dips is fun about the first two or three times and then it's not. You can't complain about a Candy Wilson spread. And you get so busy eating and laughing that you don't care what her lawn looks like or how many dust bunnies you can count if you drop one of your marbles and have to fetch for it under the couch. Laetitia said it's because Candy doesn't have anyone to keep house for, but I pointed out that that's most of us these days. If we all quit running the sweeper because we didn't have anyone else to sweep for, well, that would be a very sorry thing. Myrtle said she thought things had gotten out of shape because Candy was having trouble with her back. "Don't get me started on backs," Laetitia said. We were on a break and talking while Candy showed Alma and Birdie something about her garden, which is in worse shape than her lawn, which she would be the first person to admit. All you can see out there are weeds. I think there are weeds growing on her weeds. We talked about what hurt on us for a while, and Myrtle said we ought to all come over and soak in her new pool once she had it filled and we talked about that for a while and Myrtle thanked me for hauling away some of her cardboard, and then Laetitia brought up Candy's old friend, Irma Ray, who went out to the shed and hung herself.

Laetitia said she'd been thinking about it because it happened about a year ago. "About a year ago to the day," I said because it was. You don't forget that kind of a thing. Candy about quit club when we didn't want Irma to join. She didn't come to the next two meetings after we had our vote. Laetitia wondered if we ought to say something, since it has been a year, but I said I thought it would spoil the mood and Laetitia said I was probably right but Myrtle said she wasn't sure. I ran into Irma once at the dump. Back when Horst was still just a smear of mustard on his Daddy's sandwich. The old chiseler was talking and talking to someone I couldn't see and then it turned out it was Irma. This was back before she got fired from being a French teacher. She was always as friendly as you like. There to drop off an old mattress. Said the springs had lost their spring. Once it was out and onto the ground she jumped up and down on it a few times and said, "See, no fun." She was nice but anyone could tell she was different. And not just because she would jump on a brokespring mattress at the dump or had been all the way over to Rome. I tried talking to Candy about how she was different, but Candy didn't want to hear it. She said we were just jealous because she had a friend who didn't spend her evenings watching Vanna White mince around in her high heels. I like Vanna White. She doesn't mince. I didn't appreciate that. We hadn't finished deciding if we should say something, something nice about Irma I mean, when Candy came back in with Alma and Birdie, and even though we all looked at one another we didn't say anything. Alma stuck her tongue out at me when she came in. I stuck my tongue out back.

I called her after club and we made up. When she answered the phone she said, "Well, hello, Miss Dumbo." We're going to run over to Kokomo this weekend to visit with her niece who has some new kittens. I do not need a cat, but Alma said she might just take one and wants me to help her choose. Before we hung up she asked me what I thought about Gladys saying she had to leave early like she does about every other time. I said if I had a man who did most of his living with his head under a pillow or hiding in the closet I might get flighty too. I love Alma. We always make up. You can understand why Candy didn't want to listen to me about Irma. Everyone needs a friend. Even if the friend was a perverter of youthful morals who went out to the shed one day and put on a necktie. Hank Dunn found her. He wouldn't talk about it. Horst would make a good husband. Alma thinks he might smell like the dump when he's not at the dump, but I have never run into him anywhere else so I couldn't say. She wasn't being mean about it. We were just talking and she was just wondering. You need to tell people things. He never lets me get out of the Kingswood is something I've told Alma. He has two or three fellows who work for him now, but he always unloads my trash himself. Like a gentleman. I've asked him half a dozen times if he has his eye on someone, but he just says "No ma'am" and winks or says "No ma'am" and starts singing "I Only Have Eyes for You . . ." One time he even went into his Tuff Shed and came out with what I thought was a xylophone but that he said was a glockenspiel. It had started its days in New York City and he had salvaged it from the waste. From the waste is exactly what he said. I like a nice turn of phrase. He really is nothing like his father. He had worked on fixing and tuning it for a week. He set it up on an old dishwasher and gave me his wink and said, "Here's looking at you, kid," and right out there on the hill he played me a concert of "Somewhere over the Rainbow" and "Twinkle, Twinkle" and "Amazing Grace."

I do not mind one bit being flattered. Even if I know for a flat fact of the matter that I am ten years older than Horst's mother, who now lives year-round with his daddy down in Florida. I bet his daddy smelled when he wasn't at the dump. I bet he smells still. Down there in Coral Gables. Horst doesn't smell. I'm sure he doesn't. You can tell. I bet he showers twice a day. Jeepers. You can't salvage things from the waste and make them sound as pretty as Horst does and then go around smelling like garbage. I can't just talk about Horst with everyone. Alma is about it, which is why I did not appreciate her making loud remarks about fancy men and so on. That was going too far. She apologized for that. She said she had let the moment get away from her. And it's true. That happens. Moments do get away. I expect they are getting away from me sometimes at night when I am thinking about Horst. It's just thinking. It's not doing. Jimmy Carter was an idiot, but he wasn't wrong when he talked about sinning in his mind. You can't toss a person into the hot pitch for thinking. We're not Catholics. Not that there is anything wrong with Catholics. I don't care. Just like I didn't care about Miss Irma Ray and whatever it was she got up to in her spare time. Or who she got up to it with. I was worried about Candy was all. We've all known each other forever. Gladys is the only younger one and of course we all watched her grow up and get married and come to regret it. Well, I expect she regrets it. I've never heard her say it. She might say it to Myrtle. Although she and Myrtle aren't quite friends the way I am with Alma. Or Candy was with Irma. Still, they spend quite a bit of time together. You see them around town. Myrtle's a good influence. Gladys seems older than she is. She dresses like one of us. She's catching up.

Still, there's plenty she doesn't know. She didn't know about Noah Summers's old gal Opal, for example. You think everyone knows something, but they don't. She got Candy talking about that at the start today and Candy about wouldn't stop. I'd have thought, because of what Irma got up to in the shed, she'd have put the brakes on, but she stepped on the gas instead. Talked about how Opal burned their house down. How they weren't ever legally married. How they wouldn't let Noah in to see her when they took her up to the state hospital in Logansport. Zorrie Underwood went up to see Opal one time and came back saying she was real nice. I like Zorrie, but in my opinion "real nice" doesn't pour fuel oil all over the house, light a match, and sit down in the middle of it to let herself burn. Candy said, "I expect in Noah's mind he is still pulling her out." "But that's horrible," Gladys said. "He still loves her. He thinks they're still married," Candy said. "Well, that's a very strange marriage," said Gladys. And that stopped things because just about every lady in a visor or boa fixing to fill her belly full of pigs in a blanket and deviled eggs in that room knew more than they cared to about strange marriages. Candy and Gladys more than most.

Didn't stop Laetitia later after Gladys had left from bringing up the old one we've all heard a hundred times about that girl who fell in the gravel pit on the east leg of the Bright and about drowned only a fellow jumped in and saved her. He was so impressed by what he'd done that he got it into his head that he had to marry her. She did not share his assessment of the situation, and after he'd pestered her as long as she could stand it, she told him that she had jumped in the water in the first place hoping to drown. That in fact he hadn't saved her he had interrupted her. Thing was telling this got her kind of worked up and pretty soon they were both bawling and one thing led to another and after they'd made a night of it she said maybe they ought to get married after all. Laetitia let Alma tell the end, which was that the very first winter after they'd said their vows he went fishing and fell through the ice on the very same stretch of the Bright and drowned. All of us chipped in on the ending, which was that the widow missed her husband so much that a year to the day after he'd pulled her out of the drink she dunked herself down in it again and this time there wasn't anyone in the mood for saving her around. There's about as much made up about that story as there isn't for which the tell-tale sign is that not a one of us even knows the couple's names and everyone knows everyone's names around here, but no one said a word. I noticed Candy got quiet for a while after the second story. I don't know why Laetitia brought it up. Maybe it was her way of letting Candy know for sure and square that we all remembered about Irma.

The only other thing about club was that I managed to forget my pocketbook when I left and had to go back. Candy, who hadn't stayed quiet for long, and even there at the very end tried to get us all to dance to some of that terrible music she likes, had set it out on the front porch with a note on it that read, "I did not take any of your loot. Count it if you like!" and one last pig in a blanket in some tinfoil, which I unwrapped and ate as soon as I was back in the Kingswood. Somehow out of that I got it into my head that before I got tucked in for the evening I ought to drive by the dump again. There is a rise if you go past the turnoff where you can see the whole hill. Horst has strung up lights, which he says are for any latecomers but I think he turns them on because they are pretty. He is sensitive like that. I've heard him call his trash hill a mountain and I know he allows anyone who wants to, to sled on it in wintertime. One time last winter, after he had pulled my bags out of the back, he told me I ought to come out and give it a whirl.

I did not ever do that, but I guess I must have thought about it some because a week or so later sledding made its way into my dreams. In the dream I was on the top of Horst's snowy mountain, and it really was a mountain because when I started down I just never stopped. Whooshing down and down I went. The whole world was made of trash and snow. I had that dream several times. It was still plenty warm when I stood there looking up at Horst's hill, but I shivered. There was a light on in the Tuff Shed. There is every time I drive by after dark. I don't know where Horst gets his electricity. His father was never there after dark. Sometimes I come by late. I think most nights Horst must sleep there. He salvages a lot of things from the waste and I'm sure they keep him busy. I would like to go sledding with Horst. He says he has salvaged half a dozen sleds. When I got home and called Alma, I told her I had driven out to the dump for the second time that day. I did not tell her about sledding. About thinking about it I mean. I don't think she knows about the glockenspiel either. Jeepers, I hope Horst plays for me again. We talked mostly about Gladys. We agreed that we ought to ask her to run over to Kokomo with us this weekend to see about the kittens. She still has a lot to learn. I told Alma I would treat us all to lunch with my winnings. I really do enjoy writing things down like this. I had a teacher once who said I had the knack. She wrote that on the bottom of a paper I had written about tornados. She gave me the top grade in the class. Now I'm remembering that there was a glockenspiel in the music room at the high school. A nice girl named Rowena used to get it out and play on it. I think the teacher even let her have it. She was really good at it, could really tap the keys. One time they closed off some of the streets in Bright Creek and Rowena and some of the others played their instruments and we all danced. Now that was nice music to dance to! I wonder if Candy was there. I bet she was. Maybe it's the same glockenspiel. I doubt it but it's neat to think about. It's funny how things come back to you like that.

Gladys

The corn swallowed Gladys Bacon. It gobbled her up. One minute she was outside on the grass by the road and the next she had vanished into the green. For the first hundred and fifty yards that quick shift replayed itself in her head. There had been the summer afternoon quiet of calm breezes and far-off cars and tractors and the raspy calls of killdeer and the hum of the hot road, and then there had been the noise of her bare feet on the caked dirt and of grasshoppers clicking and whirring and of the scrape and whispery rustle of the blades of the corn stalks as she made her way past them. Gladys could hear herself clearly when she was in the corn. In that way, warm out as it was, it was a little like walking in deep winter. Like walking across the frozen world. The sound of your steps. Your breath gentling up, your heart starting to slow.

The walking generally went like this: left arm up to block the blades that would otherwise hit her face, then step, step, step,

step, step, step, step, step, step; right arm up to block the blades, then step, step, step, step, step, step, step, step. Whenever she needed to, she would cut diagonally from one row through to another. Sometimes she would cut across several at a time. Matter of fact, there were fields where almost the entire crossing was done, arm and shoulder first, on the diagonal. It depended on where she was going. Where she wanted to get. Today she was aiming to visit Mother and Daddy. Meaning there would be two fields to cross on the angle; three on the straight; and three more on the plunge. The plunge was where once she had stepped into a field and had punched in a ways, it was nothing but moving perpendicular to the rows. The plunge was done like she was swimming the breaststroke. Her hands would come up and out like she was praying and then pull apart to separate the stalks. Well, it was somewhat like praying. Like some people prayed. Usually when they were in danger in television shows and wanted to press their palms together to convince themselves and anyone who might be looking that they were right with God. Today, Gladys was slightly hampered in her passage by the pair of heels she was holding. The shoes were not a great impediment, but she wished after a while that she had gone ahead and left them behind. She had picked them out with her husband, Wendell, on one of their rare outings together and so had not been able to bring herself to leave them to lie at the edge of the field. She felt in no way hampered by the nice outfit she had on. Gladys never minded what she got dirty or what she had sweat through. She had taken off her stockings though. Cornfields—especially cornfields the day after a storm—weren't any place for a new pair of hose.

Gladys hadn't planned on setting off. Setting off hadn't even been anywhere on her mind. It was to do with how her morning with Wendell had gone plus what the girls had gotten into talking about for a while at the monthly Bright Creek Girls Gaming Club meeting she had just left. About how old Noah Summers, who lived not too far from Hillisburg over on State Road 28, had once pulled his wife out of a burning house. It wasn't to do so much with his pulling her out but more with the fact that she had started the fire in the first place. *God damn*, she had thought as she rolled out her rainbow of marbles across the Razzle Dazzle board. *God damn*, she had thought again as the numbers, most of them poor, were called out. For it had felt to her as she stood in Candy Wilson's living room surrounded by her gawdily dressed girlfriends putting on exaggerated airs and gleefully munching on Candy's snacks that she understood maybe just a hairsbreadth better than was comfortable what Opal Summers had done on that long-dead summer day. She understood it well enough that after a while she started breathing faster as she watched the others make their play. During the winter months when her breathing sped up and her heart, as she knew it was fixing to, started to thump too hard, Gladys took the edge off with half or three-quarter doses of the oval pills a doctor in Lafayette had prescribed for her, but on sunny days during the summer, when the stalks were up over her head, she went for walks in the corn. She had gotten the idea from Wendell, who during bad times overseas had sometimes curled up and slept away an awful hour in one of those far-off fields. It had come to her one day on the way to work, when she felt the familiar panic starting to rise and realized she had forgotten her pills. Instead of turning the car around, she pulled over, wandered for a while in one of Horace Allen's old fields, just walked out to the middle and back and felt better. Another day, without thinking much about it, she walked straight through the old Allen property, across four adjoining fields and found herself stepping out onto the very lane where, long before Wendell, she and a boy named Leon Stock had kissed on each other in his bright, red AMC Rambler. From then on, Gladys had walked the corn with a destination in mind.

Richie Goodwin's fields started not four hundred yards from Candy Wilson's front porch. He'd always grown alfalfa on that part of his farm. For decades he'd done it that way. But this summer he'd put in corn. She'd seen it on the drive in. And that meant, if she timed things right, and didn't mind, which she didn't, clambering over a few fences in her dress, the corn would take her all the way. So after making arrangements with Myrtle Kelly, and then fibbing to the other girls, not for the first time, that she had a stomachache, Gladys gathered up her meager winnings and her bag of marbles and went tromping off down the road. When she got around the corner to her old brown Dodge, her breath starting to go shallow, and her heart working its staccato jab on her ribs, she tossed her seventeen quarters and her game gear onto the back seat and covered them up with her turquoise boa. Then she pulled off her shoes and shucked her hose. She put as much thought as she could muster into whether she ought to hold on to her handbag, but in the end she left it behind too. She took a few steps down the rocky, prickly road toward Richie Goodwin's property line in her bare feet, thought better of it, and went back for her shoes. As was always the case when one of her walks was upon her, the closer to the corn Gladys got, the faster she stepped. It was all she could do to pause at the border and yank her shoes back off.

She never went fast once she was inside though. Inside she kept to her pace. Went steady through the green. Steady over the different flavors of dirt. In the earliest days of her time with

Wendell, she had had him show her how to march. Lord, how they had laughed as they went stomping down the road! He had learned silly marching songs in the scouts, and he had taught her those too. Long before he knew where someplace called Saigon was. He'd been sweet as a peach back then. Gladys didn't march when she was in the corn, but it was like she was marching. For there was always a schedule. Too fast or too slow, and the shadows she needed to move herself from field to field wouldn't be there. That was how she had it figured. At least her feet had to stay in shadow at all times. Otherwise it was too easy—the corn could be miles apart, and it wouldn't matter—and easy wasn't what she was after. Easy didn't ease her mind. Easy didn't interest her much at all. Early mornings and late afternoons were best. When the sun angled long and blazed everything up into a glory of green and gold. When trees and sheds and electric poles and grain bins and silos set down their blobs and bands of shade. Clear days only. That was obvious. If it was cloudy or rainy and the panic came over her, she took part of a pill or called Myrtle, and they would drive around and talk or go to the movies or stuff themselves at the Ponderosa salad bar. But the corn cure—which was what Myrtle called it—worked best.

Gladys came out of Richie Goodwin's sixty straight onto a giant shadow bridge laid down nice as you like by the plenty that remained of an old and mighty black oak. Quick climb over a beat-down fence and she was into Hank Dunn's hundred. Hank hadn't worked a field in fifty years, but that hadn't ever kept the good corn down. Two or maybe now it was even three genera-tions of Cricks had made sure his acres stayed in shape. Gladys hit the field at its northeast corner and needed to get to the southwest, so her crossing was all at the angle. The corn was taller than Richie's, and the ears were already bigger than her hands. Healthy and hard on the stalk. In Hank's field, Gladys didn't need to be as careful as she made her way forward. The angle was her favorite way to move through a field. Combination of walk and plunge. Felt like life a little. Like all the live-long days. She had told Myrtle about her corn walks. Most of the other girls would have called her crazy or even eccentric and probably tried to kick her out of club, but Gladys knew her secret was safe with Myrtle. She could tell Myrtle anything. Myrtle had a laugh on her you just couldn't keep down. When Gladys had told Myrtle one time when they were shoving salad into their mouths that she'd gotten started on walking in the corn, Myrtle had given out a happy laugh right there in the restaurant that sounded like a trombone.

"You're on the corn cure, are you?" Myrtle had said.

"Is there such a thing?"

"There is now!"

Gladys knew she could count on Myrtle to come and get her at Mother and Daddy's later. For a while it was Wendell who would come to fetch her, but apart from that one trip into Frankfort to help her buy party shoes, Wendell wasn't leaving the house much anymore.

A healthy murder of blackbirds flew fast overhead when she was about two thirds of the way across Hank Dunn's field. The flashes of red she caught as they blurred by made the sky above shine that much more blue. Farther along she spotted a turkey vulture up there riding the winds. Unlike probably all the girls in club, Gladys had nothing against the big birds. Meanwhile Wendell was downright fond of them. The presence of vultures was one of the few things that had been perfectly clear about his time "in country." There were only ever two reasons vultures came around: something was fixing to die or something was already dead. He had similar feelings about stray dogs and rats. This had got him into arguments when he was still feeling well enough to do field work. Arguments with boys who thought anything that scavenged ought to be shot. Wendell had grown up with a rifle in one hand and a shotgun in the other, but he didn't even like to hear about anyone shooting anything anymore. Some of the other veterans from around the area got up parties and went out hunting any chance they had, but not Wendell. Even hunting had turned sour for him.

Gladys's wrists and forearms were starting to chafe, and her hot, bare feet were already sweat-shod in dirt. Even if she hadn't really had a stomachache, it was true that she had eaten more than her share of Candy's pigs in a blanket, and she hadn't been anything like bashful about the sunshine salad and deviled eggs either. She loved club food. It was at least half the reason she belonged. Now, though, she was wishing she had drunk more water and less of Candy's lemonade because her mouth was all puckery, and there were still two more fields after Hank's she needed to cross before she could do something about her thirst. The first of these was a long, pure plunge south through Henry land to a shadow bridge made by a derelict hog shed garlanded by a satisfying mixture of Queen Anne's lace, thistles, shiny bright mustard, and horseweed. To some of the girls, the Queen Anne's lace and the horseweed both would have been deal breakers, but Gladys had never minded them any more than she had vultures. Things grew where they grew and flew where they flew and that was all there was to it. The dark thrown by the hog shed picked up neatly where the field shadow left off. If Gladys had come much later, she would have missed this bridge, for the sun was starting to creep and the shed was hunch-shouldered and squat. The year before, she had got caught by sudden rain close to this very shed and had crawled in among heavy coils of old wire and a set of truck tires to wait it out. This was how she learned someone kept in there a stack of girlie magazines, a pack of Lucky Strike cigarettes, and a black Bic lighter in a plastic bag. The rain had beat down long enough that day that Gladys, who had not smoked since high school, had first taken out the Luckies and lit up and then picked up one of the magazines and, squinting in the smoke, perused it. Awful thing. Pictures you couldn't get out of your head. Grinning girls with miniature waists and unholy size honkers and boy after scrawny boy with his ugly-big business pointed at all kinds of places it didn't belong. Indignant, she had told Myrtle about it, and Myrtle had laughed and laughed—about the hog shed, about the Luckies, about all of it—and after a while Gladys had laughed too.

Gladys's father had kept pictures of curvy girls on the walls of his workshop. It had been a joke with Gladys's parents that when Daddy was away from the house, Mother would sometimes take the pictures down and put them neatly stacked and tied with a pink ribbon under his pillow or arranged to look vaguely like her on her side of the bed or even, once, draped them on the Christmas tree. When Daddy got back to his workshop and discovered the theft, he would give Mother a kiss and then look until he had found them and pin them back up. Gladys's mother had always had a fine figure and had never seemed much bothered by the pallid approximations he seemed so attached to. Gladys had once asked Wendell if he sometimes looked at girlie magazines, but he had pretended not to hear. She thought that if she were a man, she would at least carry her entertainment out into the cornfield with her. You had all the privacy you wanted in a cornfield. There in the green you could plunk yourself down and gaze upon the world's iniquity to your heart's content while all the time inhaling good, fresh air. Surely a cornfield was better for the purpose than a hog shed.

It crossed Gladys's mind as she stepped off her bridge that the dark and dingy shed might be better than Vernon McKinney's field though. For once you got past the reasonable outer rows, the situation quickly devolved. Ghastly was the word that came to mind. Made you wonder if Vernon had become an imbiber or had just plain lost his taste for the farming life. It happened. Gladys hadn't passed even a single puddle or a cornstalk shorter than her own five solid feet in Hank Dunn's acreage. Vernon's was like the runt of the litter by comparison. Puddles became ponds became an honest-to-goodness lake as she cut her angle. Coming out of Hank's healthy, happy acres into Vernon's sorry ones was like stepping straight out of Candy's Lincoln into Champ Cullen's junky Pinto, which not Gladys but Wendell had more than once done. It wasn't like you wouldn't accept the ride, but, well, you took note. Wendell had said he liked Champ's junky Pinto just fine by the by, but that had been immediately after eighteen months of mud, bullets, and the aftermath of firebombs, and Gladys hadn't been a bit surprised. Her foot sank ankle deep in tickly mud, and she wondered if she ought not to give Vernon a call when she was home and make him aware that his so-called crop was better than half submerged, that he either needed to set down some serious tiling to drain it or think about turning his acres into a lake. Bring in geese and ducks. Stock it with catfish. Rent out canoes and pedal boats. Run an advertisement in the *Frankfort Times*: Come to Lake McKinney and Catch Your Supper! Or Drown!

But that was just one of those smart-ass thoughts Gladys was always having and too often felt like she needed to say aloud.

"Quips," Wendell had taken to calling them. What she would say to Alma or Laetitia or Candy or the others for the fleeting pleasure of a smirk or smile as the cards were shuffled or the marbles went clattering across the board. Wendell had used to enjoy what back then he'd called her wit. In one of his first letters home, he wrote he'd bragged to his bunkmates that his wife had a pepper shaker for a mouth. Now all he did when she tried shaking out some of that pepper for him was make a face. Still, what Vernon had done with his crop this year was a disgrace. No one could say it wasn't. Like three quarters of the county, Gladys had grown up around corn. In it too. In it every day. Played race across the rows with her best friend in elementary school, Hank Dunn's daughter Bethie. Played hide-and-seek and capture the flag with cousins. Gone out armed with hoes with her father to kill weeds. There had been acres galore to gallop across back then. Acres all her own. Well, they had been her family's. But bit by bit the Harvey acres had been sold off. Sold until there was only just one good collar's worth of crop around the house where she'd grown up, the house she and Wendell had had once Mother and Daddy had moved on. Gladys had to wait for something like fifteen minutes at the edge of Vernon McKinney's awful spread for the sun to catch the old windmill, obligingly drowned in pipevine, and send its shadow crosswise over to what had once been her farm.

Gladys stood and stared across at the land that had draped its green cape around the shoulders of her childhood and whistled a song of greeting. It was a tune Daddy had invented. I'm back, it had meant. I'm home. They had all taken it up. Gladys didn't feel sad to be whistling it at acres that were no longer hers. What was left of those acres was what had put them in the sturdy house in Bright Creek they had now. They were what had meant

Wendell hadn't really ever had to do much more after his return than occasional field work. Well, as long as she kept her job answering phones and pulling files four days a week over at Dr. Green's dental office in town. Dr. Green was a nice man. It never bothered him that she was occasionally late. He knew about the pills Gladys sometimes took, and he knew about Wendell. Everyone knew. As soon as the sun caught the windmill, she went stepping crosswise through the timothy and into her kingdom of old. Gary Falkner had done his usual nice job. The stalks weren't as tall and sturdy as Hank Dunn's but nor were they anywhere near as weed-choked or waterlogged as the travesty she'd just escaped from. Did some foxtail and ragweed Daddy would never have tolerated wave and tickle at her as she pressed past? It did. But the stalks were taut and snapped straight back to attention when you shoved on them, and the ears would soon be hard and heavy enough.

Ninety yards in, Gladys turned sharp right and then plunged twenty rows and so came to the clearing where the family house still stood. She didn't visit it every time she stepped into the corn, but today, since she was going on afterward to see Mother and Daddy, and it would be fun to tell them where she'd been, it felt right. When she stepped out of the stalks into its deep shadow on the east side, what must have been close on thirty starlings went scrabbling and cawing away from the roof. She wondered if they'd found a way to get into the attic. Had set up some kind of lunatic housekeeping now that everyone else was gone. Gary Falkner had long said he meant to make something of the place, maybe even fix it up and move into it, but every year his plough cut a little closer, and Gladys didn't doubt one day soon there would be crops growing where she and her mother and her mother's mother had once stood staring out the window, wondering when the rain would stop or whether it would ever come. The old pump was still there, too, buried in a mess of daylilies and thistles and tall grass, and she wrapped her sweaty fingers around the flaking handle. Four pulls and she was drinking and splashing. The water, liberally dosed with iron, wouldn't have won any contests for clean taste, but you couldn't say it wasn't cool. Once she had slaked her thirst and cleaned her hands, ankles, and feet, and with water still trickling down the back of her neck into her blouse, she pulled open the back door and went in. Moldy red and black carpet. Pattern she had helped her mother pick out of a catalog when the future had still seemed bright. Faded rose curtains that she herself had hung. Light fixtures filled up with flies, wasps, and those dried-up fake-orange ladybug-looking things. Her old room, site of many great plans for adventure. Mother and Daddy's room, which had then for a short time been her and Wendell's room. Big windows and a soft bed on which well before the war Mother and Daddy had fretted just too loudly about who Wendell had in the world and what Wendell wanted from the world, and into which, all of seventeen years and seven months old, she had barged and yelled, "He has *me*! *I'm* what he wants!" The mark in the west wall where not quite five years later Wendell had put his fist through the glass covering the picture of Jesus that had long hung there.

She and Wendell had emptied the house in leaving it, but this and that remained. The dinner table, which her grandfather had built and sanded and even varnished right there in the dining room, and which Gladys had not had the heart to have the legs sawed off of so it could be moved, was chief among these remnants. An armchair upholstered with the faded irises her grandmother had so loved, a rickety piano bench that had never,

at least not in this house, sat before a piano, and a pair of mysterious low stools lying on their sides up in the attic, meant either
for children or for people from an earlier, smaller age, had also
stayed. Over time, following an impulse she had never fully artic-
ulated, though she knew it wasn't just for amusement, Gladys
had carried and dragged it all to the table. She had also cobbled
together a centerpiece of dried flowers and improvised plates,
forks, and knives from bits and pieces in the cupboards and
drawers. Where something was missing, she had taken an oil
pencil and drawn it directly on the tabletop. Gladys was sure
Gary and maybe even his wife, Emma, came into the house every
now and again, but neither of them had ever said anything to her
about the strange table settings when she saw them. One of the
things she had drawn on the table was a compass she had once
owned. It had been a gift from Wendell when he left in 1968.
He had set it quivering on the table the day before he shipped
out, had told her that as long as she knew exactly where North
was, she could know where he was, which had been both
comforting and untrue. Wendell had never touched her when
he got home, but the stranger the war had made of him had
thrown her for such a loop that she had yanked the compass off
the table and taken a hammer to it shortly after his return.

Gladys sat down amid her grandmother's faded irises and
shut her eyes. Sometimes she could bring it all back. Sometimes
it returned. Mother in the kitchen. Daddy fussing away in his
shop. She didn't need any more than that. Today, though,
when she closed her eyes the first thing she thought about was
Opal Summers. Gladys didn't feel panicked anymore, but there
the old house burner was. Sitting there humming or whistling or
tapping her fingers on her own dining table as the world around
her burned. Gladys had spoken to Noah on the phone once. She

had not told the girls at club that. It was about a poem. One she
had heard Noah's late father, Virgil, recite at a Fourth of July
picnic years before. The poem was about a soaring, smashing,
sword-beaked bird, a bird made of joy, fury and hope, and when
some of its lines had come flapping their fabulous wings into her
head the morning after Wendell's nightmares had kept them
both up worrying and crying, she had picked up the phone. After
she asked Noah if he could remember the poem's title, because
she would love to find and read it, the line went dead so long
Gladys thought she had lost him, but as she was getting ready
to hang up, Noah said that, yes, he remembered it very well, that
it had been one of Virgil's favorites. In a sweet clear voice, Noah
recited the whole thing for her. She went about her business over
the following days with the electric shreds of the poem—lines
like "act, oh, air, pride, plume" and "a billion times told love-
lier" and "gash, gold-vermillion"—all a-crackle in her mouth.

Gladys had had a dream once that Wendell gave her a second
compass. He had smiled and said it was a special one that she
could use to find herself. She grabbed it out of his hand and set
out straightaway, never once looking back. She traveled north
and then west and then south and then southwest, but the dream
ended before she reached herself. Which didn't bother her. She
knew she would get there one of these times. Probably when she
was an old lady. Old like Candy. Old like Myrtle. Old like Noah
Summers. Old like her grandparents and like, she supposed,
their parents before them had gotten to be. She didn't know
much about her ancestors. Had any of them set their house on
fire? Had any of them seen the flames and gone running in?
What would the sad sack, no fun, sorry ass her husband had
turned into do if she set their house on fire? What would she do
if he did?

That morning before she left to pick up Myrtle, Gladys had tapped her head against the closet door and told Wendell that if he didn't call the number her psychiatrist in Lafayette had given them by the end of the day she would leave him. "I'm tired of waiting and I'm tired of taking pills and I'm tired of tromping around in the corn," she had said. "I know you are, Gladys," Wendell had answered. But it wasn't true. At least not the part about the corn. Not yet.

Hank

Hank Dunn's day had started elsewhere, far from thoughts of death and year-old lunches. Decent breakfast at home. Coffee at the diner in Bright Creek. Someone's sweet new wheels to whistle at. And then off. So many things to do. Even in retirement. *Especially* in retirement. This morning the main thing involved his granddaughter, Della. Crabapple of his eye. Slab of C4 snugged deep inside his skull. Della was smart as a tack and she had a mouth on her and good goddamn could she run. Quicker than snot was not an expression he favored, but he'd heard someone say it about Della that very morning at the diner and it just wasn't anything but the truth. Hank had had an earful between his decent breakfast and his coffee in town about her that morning. To do with Della and the Henry boy. To do with Hank needing to help his daughter, Bethie, rein Della in. Hank had said he would look into it. Had said he would do some talking. But not to Della. Whom he already knew had plenty of head on her shoulders. Ergo his fixing to run into town, to the Marsh grocery, where he had extracted from Tammy Henry that her son, Sugar, when he wasn't playing get-naked games with Della, had a job.

Getting himself acquainted with Della's partner in crime was his main order of business that day, but the boy's shift didn't start for a while and anyway Hank had his fields to consider. One hundred and sixty acres of Indiana prime. Not a ditch or a lane or a fence anywhere to interrupt his happy design. Half corn, half soybeans. He'd had the acreage from an aunt back when he was still running up and down the roads with a pistol on his hip. For the first years he'd just more or less let them rise and fall as they liked. But then he'd taken an interest. He had two bins in the northwest corner. Big one for corn and small one for beans. You could see all you needed to from the top of either, so he generally flipped a coin. Today the sage of Monticello decreed he climb the long ladder. This suited him fine. He might have leaned closer to ninety than to eighty if anyone had dared to count, but Hank Dunn still enjoyed his exercise. He'd had fresh gravel poured and spread just last year, so his walk to the bins came with a side of crunch. The crunch made him think of something, but he couldn't put his finger on it and it floated away. The ladder was on the shady side of the operation and the sun hadn't hit its stride anyway, so the rails were still cool. His right knee wasn't what it had once been and he supposedly had a date with a doctor who was going to enact some miracle on his left rotator cuff, but he could still work a ladder with respectable speed. There was plenty he hadn't yet given up on. If he didn't much love the short, sloped stretch with its shrinking rungs that led the last feet up to the bin's domed lid, he didn't let that stop him either. The curved metal under his butt when he sat down on it was agreeably warm. He'd sold recently, so the big chamber underneath him was empty. He smacked down his open hand and the whole thing rumbled like last night's storm. A few times, when she was smaller, Hank had let Della and some friends play kickball inside it. The sound of the ball banging on the curved metal and all that laughing had given him great pleasure.

God's country. Or God's cousin's country anyway. Maybe God's nephew. No need to get grandiose. On a clear day and with sharp eyes you could see better than five miles in every direction. Today, though, there was just the slightest touch of leftover haze in the air from the storm, and Hank's eyes, it had to be said, underwhelmed. Probably there was more weather on the way. He hoped so. The older Hank got, the more he loved the good, fresh snap of a storm. Fields and woods, houses and barns, lanes and roads stretched out around him. This had long been his dominion. His fiefdom. Funny what getting called sheriff for so many years could stuff into your head. But he and his badge had parted ways a while ago. It was like that John Prine song, the one Bonnie Raitt sang better than anyone. If his wife, Darla, who Della was practically named for, hadn't passed soon after bringing Bethie into the world, she could have said fairly about Hank for some years now: "My old man is another child that's grown old." Darla had had a fine singing voice. There wasn't anyone anything like Bonnie Raitt, who Hank had once driven up to Chicago to hear, but Darla had had a sweet, gravelly kind of alto. Everyone had said so. There was a picture of her on the mantle. Another in the bedroom. He never looked closely at her pictures anymore, but it still took him, even now, even after all these years and all the others he had tried and failed to corral, to think about her and talk to her some.

Hank could see a great cloud of starlings to the west out near
the old Harvey house and a quartet of turkey vultures to the
north. In the foreground, blackbirds with their devil-red shoulders were a little more interested in his field than he liked. Well,
let them have their nibble. A nibble never hurt. And maybe it was
caterpillars that had got them excited. Didn't matter. Hank's
acres were looking fine. They were brewing up a crop to take
all comers. Storm or not last night, there wasn't really that much
haze in the air. Hank had come back from a post-retirement
fishing trip to Alaska with a freezer full of salmon and his eyes
full of salty wet. Probably there was still some that hadn't dripped
out. One hundred miles north of Ketchikan. Water smooth as
volcanic slab. Land colored coffee and emerald. Sky like the
Virgin's robe. On the first day out, the boat had been surrounded
by gray whales. On the second they'd been courted by a lonely
humpback. On the third it was orcas hunting and playing in the
northern sun. Day after he got back, on a cool, clear mid-
September afternoon, he had climbed this very bin with a
French teacher from the high school named Irma Ray. Still
excited from his trip, Hank had told the handsome teacher about
the fancy he'd come home with. Which was that everything they
could see was submerged. That the birds were swimming, that
the browning corn was waving in the currents. That, hell, who
knew, there might at any minute be whales come swimming by.
Hank said he had told his daughter, Bethie, about it when she
picked him up from the airport and she'd said, "Oh, Daddy
Hank, you're crazy," and though probably there was some truth
to this, he wondered what a French teacher who had read all the
books and seen all the paintings and listened to all the music had
to say on the matter. Miss Ray had smiled. She hadn't said
anything for a while. Hank had liked this about her. Her slow

responses. He had liked it, not to mention the wave of her hair
and the curve of her ears, very much. The world was full of
people who just couldn't wait to open their mouths. Hank
himself was one of them. Bethie and Della too. Eventually, Miss
Ray had cleared her throat and said that she didn't know about
Hank's whales, though the idea tickled her, but that *of course* the
birds were swimming and *of course* the corn was waving in the
current. And so were they. She had disentangled her hand from
where it had been sitting in his then. She had raised it up and
then moved it gently back and forth through the air. It had been
backlit by the bright September sky. Miss Ray had asked him if
he ever climbed the bin at night to look at the stars.

"We could come back up here tonight and take a look if you
wanted to," Hank had answered. Without stopping the motion
of her hand, which she had never let him take in his again, Irma
Ray had first said, "I don't think so," and then, after only a
moment's hesitation, "What they say about me is true, Sheriff."

Or maybe she hadn't said that. Not that second part. Almost
certainly she hadn't. That had come later. She had put that in
writing. And maybe she hadn't run straight off back down the
ladder and climbed into her lemon-colored Chevy Nova and
driven away either. No doubt they had sat on up there awkwardly
for a while. Hank was pretty sure that Irma had said something
in Latin with "astra" in it. Not the familiar thing. Not the one
with "aspera." For which Hank had been grateful. You didn't
need an expression in some graveyard language to say life wasn't
easy. Hank hadn't had any durable luck in his life since Darla.
Now there was some "aspera" for you. Enough aspera to choke
on. Maybe he would tell young Sugar Henry about that. Tell him
you didn't get to pick your "aspera." Tell him it sure as shit picked
you. But he was getting carried away. Overwhelmed by interior

excess. That was something that old Virgil Summers had liked
to say about his son, Noah. Hank often quoted Virgil. He had
been quoting him for so long that Hank almost never said where
the quotes came from anymore and had no doubt garbled them
some. Was it his vision or was it his memory that was coming
up short? Why hadn't he ever taken Noah's neighbor Zorrie
Underwood up here? Zorrie Underwood had disentangled her
hand from his at the Jim Dandy restaurant. She had looked him
in the eye and said, "I'm sorry, Hank." Hank was sure that was
what she had said. It wasn't a hard thing to remember. Della
thought Hank was wise. This made him smile. The starlings
were murmurating farther away now. Over in the direction of
Gary Falkner's acres. Hank took this as a sign that it was time
to climb down.

Climbing down and then crunching across the fresh gravel—
which again made him think of something, though again he
couldn't remember what—and then getting into his cruiser and
then turning on the radio, which was set to one of Della's
stations, so that he found himself tapping a crooked finger not
unhappily on the steering wheel to the J. Geils Band, and then
heading for town, Hank thought about getting carried away.
Corporal style. Fist here. Boot there. Mostly these extremities
had been applied to inanimate objects. There were three visible
dents, for example, in this very cruiser. But he had hit people too.
There wasn't any way you could get around it. One of the people
he had hit was a vice principal. Also of the high school. This was
some while after Alaska. After the job was into the rear-view
mirror and he was riding out the long evening at Smitty's in
town. He had used to do that. Allow himself a lonely few. This
vice principal had himself an audience in the bartender, Johnny
Fearnow, and this vice principal was telling a tale. It was a tale

about following someone all the way from Frankfort to Indianapolis to see just what it was she got up to during her free time. The vice principal had recited a limerick. Hank had a bout of internal excess then.

"You won't," he said after the first punch he threw, "tell that tale," he said after the second, "again," he said after the third. But Johnny Fearnow hadn't been the first person the vice principal had sung his song to.

The J. Geils Band had given way to Survivor and then to Journey. Hank knew all the names of the bands and of many of their songs because Della just about wouldn't ride in a car that didn't have the radio switched on. When "Elvira" came on though, Hank shut it off. You could only tolerate so much corn-pone, goofball cheer. Anyway, he was there. Looked like the Marsh was doing some brisk business. Taking a turn around the lot, he spotted Candy Wilson's Buick and Lori Evans's Camaro, and Gary Falkner's little green Toyota pickup. Hank felt covetous of Toyota products. He didn't quite know why. He had done his wartime duty in the Pacific and like many in the neighborhood had held out hard against the products of the East for some years after, but then it had all broken down. Hank wasn't the only one talking up the ugly little vehicles. Bethie had a Datsun and swore by it, and just the other day he had asked Della what kind of car she had her eye on and she had said "Honda" without missing a beat. Hank meant to help her find her way into one.

SUGAR HENRY MADE things easy: he was already out in the parking lot doing a cart run.

"Della's grandpa, hop your ass in," said Hank after he had pulled up next to him and rolled the window down.

"I'm at work, Mr. Dunn, I'm working."

"Call me Hank. Take a break. They won't mind."

Sugar looked at him blankly.

"I have to clock out."

"Then by all means clock out, son."

Sugar went inside to reappear a few minutes later with Beryl Reedy, whom Hank had known for more than forty years. Beryl waved at Hank and Hank waved back and Sugar took off his work apron and handed it to her.

"Love to get acquainted," Hank said after they had rolled down 28, turned north on the old Michigan Road, then east at Central onto the Michigantown Blacktop.

"I'm supposed to be back in an hour. Two at most."

"You'll be back."

"My mother said you were going to talk to Della."

"Who says I'm not talking to her right now."

Hank couldn't tell if Sugar had taken this in or was just sitting there thinking about nothing because his face had a not-open-for-business look on it he didn't know how to read.

"How old are you, Sugar?"

"Fifteen."

"Got your permit?"

The boy indicated that he did.

Hank pulled over and got out. He walked around to the passenger side of the car and opened the door. "Slide over," he said.

"For real?"

"Is 'for real' something they're saying now?"

"I guess so. Della says it."

"Does she?"

Sugar nodded. His face still hadn't changed its expression. Or its lack of expression. Which intrigued Hank.

"Well, all right then, yes," he said. "For real."

Sugar took them straight for two miles, and though Hank had had it in mind that they would turn north when they got to a certain road and run up it to a lane halfway to Forest that would take them to a curve in the road and a bridge over a creek where in the old days he had brought no small number of miscreant county residents for "a chat", Hank decided Word of God Bridge wasn't what the situation called for and instead let the turnoff get eaten by the rearview mirror and switched the radio on. Ten or so minutes later when they had arrived back at his corn bins, Rick Springfield's "Don't Talk to Strangers," poor relative in Hank's opinion to "Jessie's Girl," was playing.

"This is Della's station," Hank said once Sugar had taken them up the lane and eased to a stop.

"I know."

"There one you like better?"

Sugar shrugged and when Hank asked him what his shrug meant, he shrugged again and when Hank said he had never learned to speak in shrug, Sugar said there weren't any good stations around here, at least not as far as he was concerned.

"But you think there are good stations, maybe on down the road somewhere?"

Sugar glanced over at him, nodded.

"Maybe up in Chicago? Or down in Louisville?"

"I don't know."

Hank put his hand on the radio dial. About a quarter of an inch down the shining silver stream he arrived at the start of 38 Special's "Caught Up in You."

"Ah," he said.

"Are we going to talk now or something?" Sugar asked.

"Aren't we talking already? Haven't we been talking since I arrested you?"

"You didn't arrest me."

"Just wanted to see if you were listening."

"I'm listening."

"It's hard to tell. You've got some Sphinx to you."

"What's a Sphinx?"

"Someone you can't figure out."

"Isn't that everyone?"

"Could be. I like that. Let's see if you can help me figure you out. You got a favorite fast-food sandwich?"

"Arby's Cheddar Melt."

"I'll add it to the list. What kind of car you after once you convert that permit of yours?"

"I like motorcycles better."

"You already know how to ride one?"

"Yes, sir."

"I can understand the appeal. You see how we're talking? I used to like to do this when I was still on the job. Kind of size a man up. Get the lay of the land.."

"When you were arresting him?"

Hank wouldn't have sworn to it, but it almost looked, no sounded, like Sugar had smiled a little when he said this.

"Sometimes," he said. "But more often when I was looking to head the need to do some arresting off. What's your favorite subject in school?"

"Math."

"What's a book you've read?"

Sugar shrugged.

"I already told you *yo no hablo* the language of shrug."

"Emerald Sylvester speaks Spanish. I heard her yelling at her husband in the parking lot the other day."

"Do you take Spanish?"

"Sí."

"Emerald's good people."

"Well, she was yelling at her husband."

"What was he doing?"

"I couldn't tell."

"We were talking about books."

"I like reading Tarzan. And Conan. And John Carter of Mars."

"Sounds like you're a reader for sure. Have you read this one?"

Hank opened up the glove box and pulled a thick book out of it and held it up. The book possessed many a dog-eared page and its cover was half torn off.

"Never heard of it."

"Now you have."

"What's it about."

"Whale hunting's the general subject. But beyond that you tell me and we'll both know."

Sugar looked at the book again. He started to shrug, then stopped and instead emitted what Hank was able to confirm this time was a little smile. "Has Della read it?"

"She said it looked too heavy to hold. You can't make that girl do anything. Don't even try."

"It looks old."

"It is old."

"She and I already talked."

"You and Della?"

"After. I mean earlier. On the phone. Before I went to work. After we saw each other in my barn."

"I heard about the barn."

"I know it."

"I'm not too crazy about the barn."

"We didn't do anything bad."

"If I thought you had, we wouldn't be sitting here discussing fine literature. You have any coins in your pocket? Random change?"

Sugar fished around in his front pocket and came out with a quarter.

"Give it a flip. Heads is the tall one and tails the short. That's the way I always do it."

"The tall what?"

Hank pointed at the bins.

THIRTY-EIGHT SPECIAL HAD stopped its cool, sweet crooning, and the next song to come on was just plain stupid-sounding, and, looking at him, Hank thought Della's beau wasn't anything like wrong to want to see what they had on offer up the road. If she had still been around, Hank might have taken Sugar over to see Irma Ray. She would have given him some things to think about. Miss Ray had seen the world. She was the reason Hank had hauled himself off to the waters of Alaska in the first place. All she had said, after listening to him run on for a while one evening in town when he still stupidly thought he was courting her, was something to the effect of, "Sounds like you're looking to drop your line in deeper waters, Sheriff," and off he, who had never traveled even much outside Indiana, had gone. To try to find those figurative waters in the literal ones. Miss Ray was long gone, but maybe when they were done talking he would take the boy over to Noah Summers's. Noah's son, Max, was visiting.

Drove an orange Volvo with Illinois plates. He'd been places too. Sugar flipped the coin. It went up almost to the sagging roof of the car but stopped just before it got there and fell.

"Heads," said Sugar.

"Get climbing," Hank said.

SUGAR WALKED SO slowly across the gravel that Hank was out of the cruiser and leaning against it and remembering now what that crunching sound was synapse-bridged to by the time Sugar had made it halfway to the bin. Circa 1940 something. He'd had business down in the basement of the funeral home in Bright Creek. Corpse to inspect. Left alone to lean over the awful face, he'd heard hollering in the next room. When his business was done, instead of seeing himself straight out, he had tried the door and discovered behind it a trine of boys in a long, narrow room holding air rifles. Or two of them were: Stephen Hunt, grandson to the funeral director, and another boy of about his vintage. And behind them little Toby Slocum with part of a peanut-butter cookie in his hand. And when Hank had taken first one step and then another, he had found himself stepping on BBs by the hundreds that had scraped and crunched between the concrete slab and his boots. "We sweep them up and use them again when we're done," said either Stephen or the other of the two older boys. They had made up a shooting range in the long room. A pair of old wheelchairs with stuffed bears sitting in them was the target. Stephen said sometimes he and his younger sister, Carolyn, got in the wheelchairs and raced around. Toby Slocum asked in a small voice if they were in trouble. "Well now, Mr. Slocum, have you committed any crimes you want to make me aware of?" Hank asked him with mock sternness. Which prompted Toby to drop his cookie and run for the darker recesses of the room. Hank followed him. And found there not a small boy to reassure but steps that dropped into a deeper basement. A woman, whistling to herself, was doing laundry in the depths.

Hank rubbed at his eyes. Out there in the clear summer air below the corn bins. It was the crunch of the gravel that had brought him to those boys and their BBs, but it was Sugar's shrugs and fleeting smiles and blank looks that had set that beauty in the basement to whistling again. As soon as Sugar touched the ladder his young body snapped to easy attention and then it was almost like he was being sucked up into the sky by pneumatic tube. Hank followed after him.

"All the way?" Sugar called down when he had reached where the ladder stopped.

"All the way," Hank called back.

The bin roof made its warm, wobbling metal sounds as Sugar scrambled up the last twelve feet. He stood a second on the domed lid before slowly sitting down.

"Quite a view, isn't it?" Hank said when he had caught his breath.

"I've been up on bins before."

"I bet you have."

Hank pointed his watery eyes out past Sugar's supposed lack of interest to the far horizon and thought of whales.

"Got a story for you."

"What kind of a story?"

"One about the old days. About back when I was young. A sheriffing story. Want to hear it?"

Sugar nodded.

"Good," said Hank with a laugh, "because I was going to tell it anyway. Cast your mind way back. To the old-timey days.

Before your parents were born. There was a killing in the neighborhood. Only one that wasn't accidental that we ever had during my time. And it fell to me to investigate. A man, so new to the county hardly anyone had gotten a chance to get to know him, got himself stabbed seventeen times and was found lying in a cold frame behind his house. You all right with details like that?"

Sugar said he was. Hank went on.

"The man lived alone on his spread about a mile out past Pickard, but he employed a pair of day workers: a hired hand and a woman to cook and clean. The hired hand was there about every day, the woman came in four times a week. On the day in question both the hired man and the woman were present. At the time of the killing the hired man had run into town to fetch some lumber to build a door and the woman was in the basement washing clothes. She was the one found the body. She was pretty shaken up. Couldn't speak at first."

Hank paused to watch a posse of dragonflies ride the breeze. He had always liked a dragonfly. Someone, sometime had told him they were good luck.

"Took a while but I did finally get an account of the morning out of her, which corroborated the hired man's story about running into town. Still, even if I wasn't any kind of a Dick Tracy about the situation, something didn't seem right about what she told me. I made inquiries that afternoon and learned she lived alone north of Tipton in a house she'd had from her family and that she was considered standoffish: better than half the time wouldn't greet you in the street. Though she hadn't seemed like anything but polite to me. I went over to ask a few follow-ups. I went, out of uniform, and that detail's important in case you're keeping track, after supper, just as evening was falling, and when she opened the door she stared at me about as blank faced as you look right now and have looked when you aren't getting that little grin of yours going since I picked you up."

"Della says the same thing. About me I mean."

"Well then it must be true. Anyway, I stood there on her front steps for about a hundred years it felt like, and then I said what I was there for and she softened up and maybe got her own little grin going and asked if I wanted some coffee. And after we had sat there a while she just more or less repeated what she had already said, and again I got that feeling I wasn't getting the goods, least not all of them."

"How could you tell?"

"Well, that's just it, or part of it: she had one."

"Had what?"

"A tell. You know what that is? It's all right to shrug now if you want to. I don't care. This is different. Go ahead."

Sugar shrugged.

"You don't know what a tell is because you don't play poker. It's a game worth playing. You ought to learn," Hank said. "I used to play a good deal of poker especially when I was still a deputy and wasn't too bad at spotting tells, and hers was that she stuck the nail of her thumb under the nail of her little finger and gave a dig. She did this at the same place in her story. It was the beginning of the story when she had left her washing in the basement to go and see what her employer wanted for his dinner. Everything after that was smooth sailing. During the tell she looked me in the eye as much as she did at any other point in the story, but at that beginning point the one nail would insert itself under the other. You get the idea? I had her go through it one last time, and when she had told it again, I said, 'Now it's time to tell me what happened before you went to see about your employer.'"

"What did she say?" Sugar asked.

"I'll get to that presently. The element of the story I will add now and that may take on resonance later is that young gal was the best-looking individual I'd ever laid eyes on, then or since."

Hank felt Sugar sit up a little, could almost feel his spine straighten.

"Got your attention, did I?"

Sugar scoffed, relaxed a little, shrugged.

"Anyway, I'll leave that portion of it for you to dream on," Hank said. "They have some pretty women over at Central?"

"Della's pretty."

"Good answer," Hank said. "This gal didn't want to tell me at first, that was clear. She was scared and after a while said so. I told her that I would help her and keep her safe, but that I couldn't do either particularly well if she didn't let me know what happened. Bear in mind now I didn't know if that was true or not. It was just something I said. I've wondered about it since. The way you wonder about things. She might have taken a good deal longer to talk and might never have talked if one of my deputies I'd let know where I was headed hadn't swung by to tell me he thought he had something. He came up to the door in his regular clothes just like I had, and she looked at him about as blankly as she had at me earlier. 'We met this morning, ma'am,' my man said. 'I know that. How can I help you?' she said. And that was when I got it. My deputy's lead wasn't all that much, but I sent him off pronto to see what he could see. I didn't need him. I knew now I had the key to the murder standing right there in front of me. We had quite a conversation she and I. I've thought of it plenty since. Here's more or less how it went."

Hank took in a deep breath, pursed his lips, and exhaled. There had been a great deal of role-playing and reenacting in his station house, and, he told Sugar, he had always been pretty good at it but it had been a while . . .

"DID HE THREATEN you?" I asked her.

And she said, "He told me he'd kill me if I talked. He had a knife. The knife. It had the blood on it."

"Who was he?"

"He was going out the side door as I was coming up from the basement. His face had a shadow on it. I didn't recognize him."

"Didn't or couldn't?"

"What do you mean?"

"I'm not sure."

"Then why did you say it?"

"Because it doesn't make any sense?"

"What doesn't?"

"Why couldn't you?"

"Why couldn't I what?"

"I *know* is what I'm trying to say."

"How do you know?"

"You can't see my face."

"Yes I can. There you are."

"What was he wearing, the man you saw?"

"A hunting coat and a red cap. It had the flaps down."

"So you couldn't see his hair. Is that how you tell people apart? By their hair?"

"I don't know what you're talking about."

"He knew. He knew you wouldn't be able to recognize him. I bet he didn't say a word, did he?"

"He . . . no."

"Not a peep, I reckon."

"He just held up the knife and put a finger to his lips."

"Who was it?"

"I can recognize people."

"Just not their faces."

"Just not their faces."

"What is it you see when you look at a face."

"A face."

"But you can't remember it afterward."

"Every face is the same face."

"What do you see when you look at my face?"

"I see your face."

"How does it look?"

"Just like a face."

"We're going to go get him."

"Who?"

"The hired man. Plain and simple. Had to have been someone who knew about your condition."

"HOW WAS THAT?" Hank asked.

Sugar shrugged. "What happened next?"

"We arrested the son of a bitch. He had a new hunting coat and red cap, and he was on his way out of town with a thick stack of stolen twenties in a leather sack. Pretty nice sack if I remember it correctly. When we had him in a cell, I went back and saw her. Even if she had had a phone, which she didn't, I would have gone out there and delivered the news in person."

"Because she was so good looking?"

"For one thing, sure, I wasn't dumb then even if I am now, but also because it makes a difference saying something when you're standing in front of someone. She told me that she hadn't been able to tell faces apart since childhood. There were clues she could use, but she still passed acquaintances with fresh hairdos and new outfits in the street and couldn't recognize them. She did it all the time."

"What happened to her?" Sugar said.

Hank suddenly realized he felt tired. Or not tired. Kind of thinned out. Probably the role-playing had done it. Or too much thinking about the past. "You ever get something wrong?" he asked.

"Wrong how?"

"Make a mistake. A bad call. Wrong when it mattered. Maybe you're too young."

"*She* did it," Sugar said.

"No, not her."

"Then who?"

"We had the right man. Right man with the wrong face."

"Oh," said Sugar.

Hank nodded.

"It's a little unexpected twist for you. She solved it and solved it right for us a few days later when she put together a packet of clothes from his closet to send over to the funeral home. Clothes fit the stabbed up man fine, shoes didn't. Shoes fit the man we had sitting in the county jail though."

"The hired man wasn't the hired man," Sugar said.

"The employer," Hank said, "wasn't the employer."

"It was the employer who knew she couldn't recognize faces."

"And the hired man who had a leather sack stuffed with twenty-dollar bills."

"Where'd he get them?"

"He wasn't what he claimed to be either."

"Is the story done?" Sugar said. "There's more to it, isn't there?"

"The more to it is the reason I thought it might be worth wasting your time up here telling it. I married her. She was Della's grandmother. Her name was Darla. Maybe all I wanted was a reason to say her name."

DESPITE HER EARLIER, unambiguous discouragement, Hank had hoped to entice Irma Ray out of the house the day he had gone to see her, soon after she had been asked to stop teaching at the high school, with the idea of sitting down over some Folger's or maybe taking a friendly walk. Instead, upon opening her door, all Miss Ray said in response to whatever exactly it was he proposed was, "I would prefer not to." They had had little contact over the ensuing years, though whenever Hank had seen her, most often with Candy Wilson, she had greeted him with a smile, and they had always exchanged a few inconsequential words. Hank had been more than a little surprised then when, not long before she put a period on the sentence of her days in the county, he received a package containing the book he now went everywhere with and a letter.

"Dear Sheriff Dunn," the letter had started. "Dear Sheriff Dunn, Do you believe in God?"

"I think so," said Hank.

"Think what?" asked Sugar.

Miss Ray's letter had been filled with talk of love, a kind of love, in no way to do with Hank, that had filled him with wonder. Certainly, what Zorrie Underwood had long nursed for Noah Summers—which hadn't been the smallest part of why she, too, had turned Hank down—was also worthy of wonder. What about what he had once felt for his Darla? Darling Darla, who had loved to whistle when she did anything around the house. Who had laughed until she cried each year when the songbirds and butterflies came back. Who had groused and crabbed and complained and then burst out laughing at herself. Darla who had kept house for a killer. Whose once-beloved face, if he was being honest about it, wasn't, like his had always been for her, anything more than a blur. Miss Ray had asked at the end of her letter if she might call him to discuss something. Something he might be able to help her with. He had called that very evening. And then he had used up the few remaining favors he had from his days as a county official to help her with her request. Bethie was the only one he had told. Candy Wilson had also been in on it. Sometimes, when he ran into Candy in town, she winked at him. Hank liked that. He liked it very much. He wished he had better understood the book Miss Ray had sent. He had read it twice. Could quote whole sentences. What weird shores we find ourselves washing up on. That was an experience Miss Ray's letter had made clear she had undergone many a time. What was it she had said to him about aspera? He was glad he had helped her. He said as much. Aloud he thought but Sugar didn't seem to have heard him and just said, "I need to get back."

AND LATER THAT afternoon when sudden pain in Hank's arm bloomed and spread to encompass the whole of his chest—as having returned Sugar to the Marsh after a short stop at old Noah Summers's place, where they had found not Noah but his son, Max, who had quietly shared a few choice anecdotes about the great, wide world, he rolled alone down 421 toward Bright

Creek—it was of Irma Ray's letter that Hank thought. Or, more exactly, it was of the fried egg sandwich he had slowly eaten as he read.

Came into his mind the crispy firmness of the white and the tender yellow of the yolk. Came into his mind the whipcrack tang of the horseradish without which any fried egg sandwich had always struck him as a pitiable thing. Came into it how every few minutes he had dipped his fingers into a bowl of wonderfully greasy corn chips he had set out earlier that day for Della, who had not touched them for fear they might come back to haunt her on the track. Came last, though hardly least, how without much paying attention, barely taking his eyes off Miss Ray's words, he had several times licked clean his fingers during that simple but satisfying meal. "Interesting thoughts on your cetaceans in the enclosed," Miss Ray had written in an understated postscript to the letter, which itself, it struck Hank as his car crossed the center line, had been anything but.

Irma

Dear Sheriff Dunn,

Do you believe in God? In the Good Lord, the Heavenly Father, the Almighty, the Great (as my old granny used to call Him) Amen? I ask because the question has been troubling me recently. Not troubling me to distraction, you understand, but troubling me just the same. I'm not even sure you would call it a crisis of faith. But it's something. I still believe. I'm sure of that. But I'm not always sure just what or which parts I believe in. Joy? Sure. Love? Without question. Beauty? Uh huh. The peace which passeth all understanding? Count me in! But the rest of it? Who knows? I guess, if you can stand me quoting Elvis, "I'm all shook up." How are you fixed with it all these days? I should warn you: this is not an innocent question. When we were spending time together you referred to yourself more than once as an agnostic. And agnostics, if I'm not mistaken, don't let themselves get bogged down by the details. This is good.

For the longest time I thought the Good Lord was an all or nothing proposition. You took It or you left It (It never left you). Agnosticism was just the coward's way out. I wonder if that's what I've become. A coward I mean. How things change. When I was a small girl, my belief was extreme, and took extreme forms. Once for example I became confused enough by something said on Sunday about the omnipresence of the host that I filled my breakfast bowl with what I thought must be holy dirt from the back garden, covered it with mashed zinnias and ate the mixture, every rock, petal, chipmunk turd and crumb. Is this a fit line of inquiry (and appropriate register of utterance) for a letter to a retired public official? Even one I once counted as a good friend? I hope so. I would hate to think I'd lost you before I'd said anything that wasn't disagreeable, sentimental or dumb. It's all a risk though, isn't it? Just writing you this letter is a risk. I rejected your kindness in the past and (I blush) quoted the author of the book I enclose here as I did so. "I would prefer not to." How insufferable I can be! Already this letter is a mess and it's the third time I've tried to start it. But I'm moved to beg a bit of your kindness of old and for that I need to offer you some context. I don't see any way around it. I'll keep on.

When I was older and began to settle on my first true loves, which were movies, and practically every single person bad or good in them, I thought what I was feeling must surely be Divine, and it was the same way with books and paintings (the older the better from the start). Probably I loved music most of all and though I wouldn't cast aspersions on the piety of my peers I don't doubt that mine were the only twelve-year-old eyes that grew moist at the United Methodist church I attended whenever we were asked to open our hymnals and turn to the "Old Wooden Cross" or "How Great Thou Art" or "A Mighty Fortress Is Our God." Those workaday devotionals, which a whole great corner of the country will go to the grave being able to hum, represented a kind of apotheosis, a wedding of music and belief in the Great Amen's glory. It didn't matter a bit that the parents and siblings on either side of me were to a one barely on the blessed side of tone deaf, even as they offered up what must have been the entire contents of their lungs: the effect on me was entirely convincing, even, at times, overwhelming.

I think it would be fair to say that during those early years, if ever an angel had appeared to me in my back yard while I was playing at this or at that, and had told me to raise an army to fight the English, or leap from the town's tallest building (which would have been our hideous courthouse) for that matter, I would have done so. But it never happened. The years went by. I saw no angels. The fever broke. By high school I had become at best a Sunday Christian. Something I had previously despised. I kept on at church and attended the occasional adjacent after-school activities, which involved much more baking and smiling than I liked. But that was all. And then I met someone. This was at Earlham. We were in classes together. We joined several clubs. She was studying music. There I've said it. What they say about me is true, Sheriff Dunn. You've heard it from the horse's mouth. She was a couple of years ahead of me. We fought too much. It didn't last. But then much later our paths crossed again. First in the faculty lounge at the high school here (she had already been the music teacher for a decade) and then as we blushed in our Sunday best in the north aisle of the Bright Creek Assembly of God. Blushing because we had both sworn off God and church forever with all the undergraduate earnestness that had been ours and now, well, here those years later, modest, school-teaching, lower-case christians, we had become. "It just appealed," she said. "Also the weekends are dreary." I understood that. The world had changed. They were dreary. And we weren't discussing Diderot or Simone de Beauvoir at Earlham anymore. We continued the conversation over turkey melts at the diner. She invited me over a few days later to listen to her records. It was an extraordinary collection. Some of which dated back to those freer, easier, practically communist days we had known. It was nice to think about those days. It was also nicer than either of us thought it would be to meet again. Eloise was her name and she was persuasive. I didn't need much persuading but she was. After a few years she inherited some money and quit teaching and moved to Indianapolis, which made many things easier.

She got tired of church again but I didn't. I'd go down to see her after school on a Friday and be back early Sunday to bow my head and raise up my voice. This wasn't anything to do with repentance. Let me be clear as crystal about that. I have my faults, grudge-holding for one, but neither Eloise nor any of the others (yes there were others after Earlham) are among them. Also, much as I enjoy it, I don't sing very well. I'm not much better than my above-maligned family. Eloise is the one with the voice. And you should hear her at the piano after she's had a glass of wine. Do you remember how much I enjoyed a glass of wine? Well, she is the one who taught me. We've seen things. We've traveled together. I told you about some of those trips. I apologize if I implied that I was alone on them. Eloise isn't always nice but I've never doubted. I'm sorry you got to liking me so much, Sheriff Dunn.

I'm sorry too though in a different way that Bob Barlow, Vice-Principal at the high school (I *know* you know about him), got to liking me too. He tried it out with half the female faculty at school, my dear Candy included, without much fuss when his advances were spurned, but there must have been something about the way I told him (en français, which as former head of the languages department he understood perfectly) what I thought of his invitation to attend a hog auction, if you can believe it, that convinced him he needed to follow me one Friday afternoon and to come back squealing (or do I mean oinking?) about what he saw. Candy and I blacked our eyes, put on bala-clavas and took some teenage revenge on him a few days after my dismissal when there was a game on. And I know you punched him one night on my behalf. Which is part of the reason I'm writing to you now. That you did that. Do you know who told me? Principal Markson. He called me up and said that you had smacked Bob around pretty hard. That you had done it for telling tales about me at a bar. The good principal then opined that for someone whose tastes ran in such "a different direction" I sure got "the fellas" worked up. "Such a waste," he added. You could hear his chair creak as he said this. He always liked leaning back when he had you in his office. He then made the speech, one I'd had a hundred times already from my poor parents (and two poor aunts and one poor uncle), about how it wouldn't end well for me if I stayed on "this path," that stories like mine were always sad ones. Ugh. That odious certainty. Pathetic. I told him I had thrown up a little in my throat while he was talking, and then I called him what I had called Bob Barlow (though en anglais this time), and then I hung up on him.

You would truly never know it to look at me (I believe you occasionally called me Mother Teresa), but I have always wanted

to punch someone. I think I would be good at it. If you and I had
stayed close I might have asked you to give me a few tips. Still,
there are all kinds of ways to strike. I learned this early. It wasn't
all bowls of dirt and caterwauling at church during my childhood. My mother set the tone. She liked to play silly tricks on
my father. She would put sardines in his sandwich or vinegar in
his water or jelly up the handle of his toolbox or shortsheet his
bed. He loved it. Told everyone proudly that she could have been
a clown. Told her to never, which she didn't, stop. "Don't go
overboard" was her sage motto: it wasn't buckets of water rigged
above doorways for her (I tried that once on a bully of a professor
at Earlham with mixed results). "A little salt in the sugar bowl
goes a long way" was another thing she would say. Her grandfather, my great-grandfather, who was a presbyterian preacher
known to read the spines off his bibles, would fire his rifle out
the window whenever he or someone in the family got good
news. That lodged in my head too. I have never owned a gun
but I have always kept the firecrackers figuratively *and* literally
close. Which reminds me that the Fourth is coming up. The
Fourth is my favorite holiday. Always has been. I'm about as
patriotic as an over-ripe pumpkin but I do love a good, loud,
long, lovely light display. I make Eloise drive over to Ohio every
year with me so I can load up on bottle rockets and roman
candles and as many explosives as she'll let into the car. This year
was no exception. I'll toss an M-80 next week in your honor,
Sheriff Dunn. At any rate, some of the ancestor-inspired
"punching" I got up to after I was essentially fired involved those
balaclavas and toilet paper. Some involved glue, toilet seats and
(my mother would not have approved) tacks. Do you know that
certain of my former students took to wearing berets to school
and speaking only in mock French accents in solidarity after I

was fired? It caught on. One day half the school put on berets
at assembly and the ring leaders, who wore their subsequent
suspensions like a badge of honor, hollered out "Mon dieu!,"
"Sacré bleu," and even "Au diable, connard!" when Bob
announced an immediate ban on berets. You guessed it, the beret
and accent protest was my idea. Mine and Eloise's. We came up
with other things too. Modest pranks and capers. Don't worry:
I never did anything like cut Vice-Principal Barlow's brake cords.
And it's fine now. That's passed. Or mostly. Eloise says I hold on
to things. She says it's very un-Sunday-christian of me. I suppose
it is. Nonetheless I would have likely eventually started letting
it all slide off my oily feathers only there was also Principal
Ransom. And plenty of my former colleagues. And there were
the parents. Oh, the parents. If I've had a trickle of private
students since my dishonorable discharge it has had only to do
with the insistence of their offspring (the beret-sporting ring-
leaders). Word apparently got out that Miss Ray would teach
them things at her house that she could never have done at
school: how to say all the sweet Gallic nothings and swear en
français like sailors and regale them with racy stories about
Rome and Paris and New York and Budapest and play them
Juliette Gréco or Françoise Hardy and show them how to tie a
silk scarf to best advantage and pass them interesting, inappro-
priate things to read. Very little of this was true, Sheriff Dunn.
I'm actually a very boring kind of a teacher. I've had to be. And
not just so that no one would *ever* suspect me of pulling the occasional prank. I'm sure you understand me. Still, I did, against my
better judgment, sometimes loan books to my best students. And
have also paid the price. I was just the other day yelled at in
K-Mart by a mother about, of all things, *Bonjour Tristesse* by
Françoise Sagan. Her daughter was my final student. There

won't be any more. That's okay. I'm sick to death of it. Of all of it really. Eloise has long thought me mad to stay on here. I can't tell you how many times she's suggested I see a psychiatrist. I haven't. And I really couldn't tell you why I've kept living here for so long. I've got Candy of course. But the gaggle of old geese (gah, I'm an old goose too) she's known her whole life, have never done more since my fall than tolerate me. Candy has tried over the years to bring me back into the fold. It has not gone well. Though it has sometimes been amusing. And revealing. Those old girls play at dress up every chance they get. And wear their costumes awfully convincingly.

But I digress. Again. I suppose what I'm trying to say is that my tender, tricksy heart has been bruised during my time here. It has been hurt. It hurts now. That's true. Ouch. And you know now how I react. Which is why I'm hoping when you are finished with this letter instead of calling the Logansport State Hospital and telling them they need to come down and collect me (my father, bless his heart, once threatened me with conversion) you will call me. Candy's already said yes, by the way. So it can't be too completely crazy, can it? Well, maybe it can. For her part, Eloise does. not. approve. She says it's too much. And probably illegal. And that no one will understand. Because none of them will know. But *I'll* know. I got the idea last week after church. The sermon had revolved around the resurrection. Which the same old Granny I evoked at the start of this interminable screed—the one who called God the Great Amen—always referred to with admiration and just that touch of envy as the Great Escape.

Thinking of this, I drove into Frankfort for a Coke and hot dog on the square and bumped into an old friend of yours, Zorrie Underwood, as I sat munching on a bench by my car. I do not know her very well, and only through Candy, but she was coming up the walk and there I was and she has never not said hello when I'm alone like so many around here and so we visited for a while. The conversation took us to the time during the Depression when she found work daubing clock faces with radium paint over in Illinois. Did you know about that? She didn't say nearly as much about the horror of that work as we understand it now (though she mentioned a friend she'd lost) as she did about how marvelous she and the other "ghost girls" felt after a long day as they went along glowing together through the dusk an image that curiously (fortuitously?) reminded me of an evening in a little village north of Florence in far off Italy where I long ago arrived after dark and felt so at home amongst its scattering of twinkling lights that I exclaimed aloud to those I was traveling with (how they laughed at my exuberance and at the idea's improbability) that one day I would come back to live there! Mrs. Underwood and I then talked about you for a while—which made it clear to me that she and I had a thing or two in common—and then about the weather I suppose and then we were done.

As she walked off two things came back to me. One of them was your imagination. Which was never more in evidence than when you told me on top of your corn bin that time about how you had taken to imagining there were whales swimming above the fields. The other was an image you shared with me as we stood outside the Red Barn theater after *Oklahoma!*, or was it *Damn Yankees!*? to do with an arrest you had once been obliged to make around Rossville. You told me that the woman, a bank teller in bad trouble for embezzling, whom you found in her front room with the door standing wide open, was so absorbed in teaching herself the steps to a jig that she didn't notice you looking in through her screen door, while you, for your part, were too amazed by the spectacle to interrupt it and ended up tiptoeing off and leaving the arrest for later. I had the taste of mustard in my mouth as I sat there thinking about you doing that.

In Friendship and with enduring fondness (please do call me),
Irma

Ps. Interesting thoughts on your cetaceans in the enclosed.

Myrtle

Myrtle could not for the life of her understand why Gladys Bacon's Dodge smelled like Christmas oranges. She had noticed it straightaway when Gladys picked her up to go to lunch and then again when they had left the Ponderosa to drive over to Candy Wilson's for club, but both times they had set straight into talking and now of course Gladys could not be asked because Gladys was gone. Myrtle gave a sniff over her shoulder in the direction of the back seat, where Gladys's gaming vestments and accoutrements lay strewn, and then leaned over and smelled at the dash. It was definitely coming from the front half of the car. When was the last time she had smelled Christmas oranges? You hardly ever saw one anymore. Was it just clove she was smelling? She turned around and sniffed at the leather seat back. No, there was definitely citrus in the mix. When Myrtle leaned forward to try to get her nose closer to the instrument panel, she bonked her forehead a good one on the top of the steering wheel and she laughed. It was just a quiet laugh. By Myrtle's standards. Myrtle never chuckled. She never tittered. Something was either funny or it wasn't, and if it was funny, she laughed out some subset or combination of hard, loud, and long.

Laughing, she tabled the question of where the smell was coming from, grabbed Gladys's turquoise boa off the back seat, untangled it from the pair of L'eggs it came with, laughed harder, draped the boa over her shoulders, put the key in the ignition, and, still laughing, drove off. She honked when she passed the cornfield she knew Gladys had gone into for her walk. Gladys had left the meeting over an hour before and would have long put this first field behind her, but it was fun to honk anyway. Nobody else at club knew what Gladys was up to, and Myrtle liked being in on it. The plan was she would pick Gladys up a little after sundown at the cemetery. Her walk had to be done by then. Gladys had worked up all kinds of things she could and couldn't do on her walks. There was a lot to do with angles and timing and something Gladys called shadow bridges between fields. Myrtle knew of about seven of these walks. Probably there had been more. When she picked Gladys up, she would ask her what fields she had passed through, what she had seen. Sometimes she had seen funny things: towers made out of tires painted with polka dots, or Meg Falkner's three-legged ewe doing tricks with a ball, or stashes of sexy magazines.

In the meantime, what a day! Myrtle hadn't had so much fun at a club meeting in many a shiny moon. Candy knew her business when it came to the kitchen. Plus Myrtle had won twenty-seven dollars and fifty cents. The haul was crinkling and jingling in her purse. Never mind that she hadn't been the big winner of the day. That honor had gone to Lois Burton, who would be riding home with a cool thirty-four dollars. But twenty-seven dollars and fifty cents wasn't anything to sneeze at. Myrtle thought first thing she'd do was use a little of it to buy a couple of cold ginger ales. Take them when she went to pick up Gladys. Gladys hadn't gone overboard at the snacks table like she had, but she'd gotten in there. Gone after those pigs in a blanket. Snacked down her share. None of the girls would say no to some good cold ginger ale before bed this evening. No, they would not. And Gladys, whose own meager winnings lay in a little silvery puddle on the back seat, would be extra thirsty after all her carrying on in the corn.

Only it was over two hours until pick up. Myrtle thought first maybe she'd just as well pass them with the help of *Wheel of Fortune* or *Jeopardy!* back home, but when she leaned over to turn on the radio she caught another whiff of that Christmas tang, and though she still couldn't understand why she was smelling it, it brought something back to her. A minute went by before she could figure out what it was. During that minute it felt like running into someone she'd once known better than anything in the world but suddenly couldn't place. This had happened to her several times in recent years. For instance, a few summers before at the county fair she'd chatted with a bearded and behatted grandpa for half an hour before realizing that sitting there before her was the wintry dregs of the boy on whose smooth and pretty cheek she had bestowed her first romantic kiss. It was as she was thinking of that beau—who had confessed to her huge laughter that he hadn't been able to place her either—that it came to her. She turned off State Road 28, ran south for some miles, then east along a little dirt lane that had seen better days, until she had pulled up at a big, blank rectangle of grass surrounded on three sides by soy beans where the schoolhouse of her youth had once stood.

She climbed out of Gladys's car and stepped a few feet into the tall grass. Got herself oriented. The front of the building had faced west. No, of course it had been east. There had been windows on the south side. She went in through what would have been the front door. Presently she was standing inside. Presently she was walking down the center aisle between the desks. Presently she was waiting none-too-patiently for Miss Pearson to look up from the papers she was grading at her lectern and ask her what she required. It was a cold day. The little stove in the corner was never quite up to the job. Myrtle had marched fast through the dark and snow that morning because of the Christmas orange she now had in her hand. She and her grandmother had made it the night before to take to Miss Pearson as a present. When Miss Pearson looked up, she seemed annoyed. It was true that Myrtle was often away from her desk, much of the time when she shouldn't be. Also, Miss Pearson thought her laugh was far too loud for such a little girl in such a little countryside schoolhouse. Myrtle had done her best to laugh quietly but her best had just not been enough. Now Miss Pearson was looking at her with an eyebrow raised. She was saying "Well, what is it, Myrtle?" And Myrtle was blushing and handing her the Christmas orange. And Miss Pearson was taking it and giving it a quick glance and saying, "Ah, thank you, Myrtle," but still looking annoyed, still with that eyebrow raised. Myrtle saw her Christmas orange in the trash later that afternoon when she went back for her forgotten bag. She plucked the orange out of the trash and cried a little and then spat on it and threw it into a snowy ditch on the way home. The orange looked very bright half buried in the snowy ditch and she almost went down to fetch it. But in the end she left it there to freeze.

Just like when the school year was over Myrtle left her final
assignment stay where it was instead of picking it up and turning
it in. Miss Pearson made a fuss about it and, because of Myrtle's
poor to middling grades all along the line, only a long talk with
Myrtle's grandparents convinced her to pass Myrtle on to middle
school. The assignment was about the cycles of weather in the
county. The weather was Miss Pearson's great subject. She often
said that it wasn't the look of the land that mattered about a
place, it was the feel and effects of its weather. The students had
consequently spent more time with charts and maps to do with
meteorological phenomena than with any other subject. The
barometer that hung on the north wall was inspected daily. Once
the older kids, including Myrtle, climbed a ladder to the top of
the schoolhouse to try and spot a tornado somewhere over by
Sheridan, but all they saw was enough lightning to make Miss
Pearson call for them to climb back down. There was a lesson
on mercury, on its globbiness and peculiar tendencies. They
learned how much of it lived in the class thermometer, which
they were often sent out with to get readings on different parts
of the school grounds.

Weather wasn't monolithic, Miss Pearson liked to say. The
weather changed with every step and every minute. Weather
touched on different subjects, on history and mathematics and
English. She liked to talk about the importance of mathemat-
ical formulas for a meteorologist. She pointed out that history's
greatest philosopher, Aristotle, had written a book called *Mete-
orology*. They studied clouds, they studied mist, they talked about
the global impact, influenced by weather, of the 1883 explosion
of Krakatoa. Local weather events caused by the temperature of
the far-off ocean came up frequently. Myrtle's final project was
about the wind. Miss Pearson showed them how they could use

a special sock to measure its speed, and Myrtle sewed one with
her grandmother's help and then went to six places twice daily
for a week and recorded the result. She made an illustrated map
with water color and colored pencil that she called The Winds
of Bright Creek. Miss Pearson saw it in its earliest stages and
was most excited. Thinking back on it, Myrtle felt sure that it
was this very excitement, which was so at odds with Miss Pearson's reaction to the gift of the orange, that had made her
decide to take it out to the shed and hide it behind a stack of
old siding rather than turn it in. No one believed that she had
lost it, as she claimed.

Funny thing was, sixty-five years later Myrtle knew exactly
where the assignment was to be found. And it hit her after she
had exited out the long-vanished front door and walked back
through the warm timothy to Gladys's Dodge—where she found
that the smell of Christmas orange had grown, not diminished—
that there might be worse things in the world to do with a
couple of quiet hours than "make good," as her grandfather had
suggested when some years after she was out of school entirely
and already married, he had discovered the assignment, dusted
it off, and brought it to her. "Well, I don't care if she was mean
about your orange," he had said when she had given her
reason for not turning it in. "There's life a lurk behind all of us.
Even schoolteachers. You'll see. Maybe she'd had a fight that
morning. Hell, maybe her dog had just died." Myrtle, who had
by that time already had a taste of how feckless a fine-looking
young husband could be, had a good idea about what her grandfather meant by life being a lurk. Still, she had not made good
and then the years had gone by, and her grandmother and
grandfather not to mention that feckless husband of hers,
whom she had ended up loving plenty, had died, but not Miss

Pearson. Miss Pearson, a young woman when Myrtle had been her student, was now over at Wesley Manor in Frankfort. Myrtle still had a good piece of those two hours to play with. So why not? She was already dressed for visiting.

From her front porch, Myrtle spotted something shiny leaning up against the brand spanking new above-ground pool she'd had put in as grandchild-bait but hadn't yet filled. Taking a minute to inspect, she found an unopened bottle of Coke, no longer cold, next to an empty bottle set to lean companionably close. So she knew that handsome Horace Allen had stopped by. Made sense that he'd come over to have a look at the pool. She'd bought it on an impulse, hadn't told anyone she was doing it, but you couldn't keep something like that secret in Bright Creek. Maybe it was time to fill it. Maybe she would take a dip. Maybe Gladys would want to. You couldn't wait on grandkids who weren't coming forever. She uncoiled her hose, draped it over the pool edge, turned on the spigot, picked up the bottles and then went into the house through the back door. On the way out again with the wind map under her arm, after she'd dropped the one bottle in the trash compactor and popped the other in her fridge, it occurred to her that she might ask Horace if he'd like to ride along with her to the Manor, that it might be just the lark he was looking for. But it had been a long time since they'd gone somewhere together in a car, and even if it wouldn't be awkward for her it probably would be for him.

She'd wrapped the map up in brown paper and tied it with a green bow. It was a little bulky in the frame her grandfather had carefully made for it all those years before because he had been so proud of her work and thought it merited proper display, but it still fit pretty well under her arm. Maybe Miss Pearson would have a place in her room at the Manor where she could hang or lean it. Or maybe when Myrtle had left, if old as she must now be she couldn't do it herself, she could get one of the aides to toss it, too, into the trash. Myrtle laughed at the idea. Indeed, she had to lean a minute against the hood before she got back into Gladys's car. Ordinarily she would have taken her own, but the garage door was fussy and she was worried if she took the time to fight with it she might run short. Anyway, Gladys wouldn't mind. She was a good egg. It wasn't just any old chicken that had laid her.

Myrtle tuned the radio to the classic country she favored and let first Kenny Rogers, then Patsy Cline, then June Carter Cash followed by Willie Nelson serenade her over to Frankfort. Once she had arrived, she sat a minute in the car until "Always on My Mind" was through. She hadn't ever loved all of what Willie had put out to the public, but this new one was special. She whistled a little of it as she carried the map across the parking lot. Myrtle's whistling wasn't any great shakes. But it was adequate. She could mostly carry a tune. Going up the walk to the building where she thought she too might one day soon have to park her carcass, and thinking about where she was supposed to pick up Gladys later, there appeared before her a vision of a mason at work on her stone. "MYRTLE EDITH KELLY" he would chisel. Her mortal dates he would chisel. "SHE WAS AN ADEQUATE WHISTLER" he would conclude. Myrtle was still laughing about that one when she went in the first set of doors, but she had settled herself down by the second. There were times people had taken her for a drinker. A drinker or crazy. But she was neither of those things. Self-control was something she had cultivated, something she prided herself on. The girls at the club had nothing to complain about in that regard. It was true, though, that she sometimes had to work at it. Which was definitely the case as she stated her business at the front desk—to pay a call on Mrs. Winnifred Pearson Baker—for she could see in the big mirror behind it that she had forgotten not just to remove the turquoise boa but her grandmother's old paste tiara too. She mastered herself quickly enough in part with a quick chomp on the inside of her left cheek (she alternated) but wondered if the memory of what she had seen in the mirror and the oddness of her errand might yet successfully conspire against her despite her resolve. For his part, the man who greeted her must have seen it all when it came to gaudy cheer, for he said not a word about her appearance and responded to her over-sober and probably unnecessary remark that she'd been at a club meeting only by smiling with the half of his mouth that didn't have a cigarette dangling from it and asking her to grab herself a seat in the next room.

The room was large and the wait long. Myrtle had imagined that she would be surrounded by local denizens, had thought of a few she was likely to recognize, but there must have been bingo or a dance class or something else popular going on, because apart from a man who drifted along the hallway with a walker and someone flanked by a pair of younger intimates out in the yard, she spied no one who didn't look like they worked there. She passed the time counting things like potted actual plants and potted artificial plants and portraits of Jesus and the angels and many slogans about grace and good cheer. There was a photograph of Ronald Reagan on the wall. Myrtle was not a big fan of political displays. She had never found Ronnie handsome and did not think he had aged at all well. At one point she got up to better see the words on a poster about invisible footsteps. The room was clean. The visiting table she sat at had been recently polished. No AC but the fans they had running seemed to be keeping the situation under control. There was an abundance

of Bibles and back issues of the Upper Room, and board games
had been stacked in good supply on another shelf next to plenty
of decks of cards, some in boxes, some wrapped tight with rubber
bands. Razzle Dazzle didn't feature in the public offerings of
course, but that didn't mean when the hankering came on you
couldn't invite some girls over to your room and play a few
rounds.

Most of the girls at club talked about transporting their
pillows permanently over to the Manor before long. Some had
even put together their down payments. Gladys of course didn't
take part in these conversations because Gladys was still too
young. No need there for an exit strategy. Unless it was from her
marriage. Her trip to earthly happiness with Wendell Bacon
hadn't started out all that well, in Myrtle's opinion, and then
there about hadn't been anything but flat tires, bad exits and
wrong turns. Myrtle placed the blame squarely on Wendell but
probably that was unfair. She had talked about it with Horace
a number of times. Horace said that what Wendell needed was
help. And Horace ought to know. Horace had fought in the big
fight. Had got himself half killed in it. Had found a way to fall
in love. He had never actually come out and said it when they
were keeping company but she had figured it out. That he was
pining. That between her heart and his stood a whole pine forest.
She'd kept trying anyway. Handsome Horace. He'd been awfully
pleasant to cuddle with. Nice manners too. You took what you
could get and sometimes it was enough and sometimes it was
not. Gladys had chosen to wrap her arms around a man with
already depressive tendencies who'd volunteered for Vietnam
and come back practically carrying himself in his own suitcase.
Oh well. Miss Pearson had also had her adventures in love.

Matter of fact, when they finally rolled her in, Myrtle was thinking about how Miss Pearson had fled the county not even a year after turning her nose up at that poor old Christmas orange, how it had been whole decades lived down around Evansville before her fine and fancy man had shucked off his mortal coil and she'd moved back. Straight to the Manor. Like she'd been shot out of a gun. Myrtle had spotted her a time or two in recent years at this or that event, had even once introduced her to Gladys.

"Hello, Winifred," she now said.

"You'll have to say it louder," said the attendant before setting the wheelchair brake, patting Miss Pearson on the hand, then making for the door.

Miss Pearson had on a bulky green cardigan even though it was July. She had on a heavy, brown wool skirt and saggy hose. The hose were the kind you weren't supposed to be able to see through. They had clearly not been made by the same company as the ones out in Gladys's car. Myrtle faced a few seconds where she had to stifle another laugh because she suddenly thought what if Gladys's L'eggs had stayed caught up in her boa? What if that was what she had spotted in the mirror? What if that was what the man at the front desk had been tasked with contemplating? A quick chomp on her inside right cheek helped the moment pass.

"Hello, Winifred!" she called.

Miss Pearson levered up her forearm and waved. Myrtle thought she was looking good and said so. Didn't matter one bit that Miss Pearson's mouth hung open and that her tongue, bulging a little, was visible behind her bottom dentures. Truth be told, Myrtle had lately started to catch her own mouth coming open when she hadn't invited it to. Generally, it was when she was working on something. Matter of fact that very morning while she was spooning sugar onto her oatmeal she'd felt some breeze on her teeth. Some of the girls made self-deprecating jokes about how their faces were turning into fly catchers, but Myrtle had never minded that look. Both her grandparents had worn it plenty as they were rounding the final bend. Myrtle thought it made a person appear astonished. Like they were thinking on some great wonder. Something marvelous. A memory they were the only ones in the whole big world to have.

"I came to make good, Miss Pearson!" Myrtle called. And when the old lady squinted her eyes and frowned a little as if she hadn't understood, Myrtle said, "I know your last name isn't Pearson anymore. I know you got married. I know you're not a 'Miss.' It's what I called you when you were my teacher. When I had you at school. And I'm here about that. It's the reason I came."

Miss Pearson nodded. Her mouth had closed but now it came back open. The buckled shoes her hose were bunched against did not move, like they had been fixed by glue to their footplates.

"I've got my assignment, Miss Pearson. That one I never turned in. I'm sorry it's so late."

Myrtle now picked up the package containing the framed map. She wondered if she ought to undo the ribbon and tear open the paper but worried that to do so might seem condescending. Her own grandmother had hated it there at the end when Myrtle had offered to button her buttons and tie her shoes. Didn't mean she hadn't let her. But it had made her mad each time. It was better to wait to be asked. To wait until someone was ready to raise the white flag. Generally, was her experience, people surprised you. Her grandfather for example had one day simply tossed the keys to his beloved truck across the room to her, had said his driving days were done, that he would call her up if he needed to get somewhere he couldn't walk to.

"I know it's silly, Miss Pearson, but it came to me this afternoon and I remembered where it was and I thought I'd go ahead now if you don't mind and turn it in. It was about that orange I gave you, not that that matters anymore. Some old orange. I mean why I didn't turn it in to you when it was due. You can grade it if you want. I mean when you've had a chance to look at it."

Miss Pearson said something then or tried to but no sound came out.

"It's about the weather. About the winds around Bright Creek. My grandma helped me make a sock to measure them. Remember how much you liked the weather? I think it was your favorite thing in the world."

Myrtle tapped the package. The paper must have been stretched extra taut across the hollow of the frame because the sound made Myrtle think of a snare drum and the effects she sometimes still heard on the radio during certain advertisements. She had dated a fellow not long after her husband's death who had done that kind of work. He had a practice area in his back room. Myrtle had taken a turn. She had enjoyed approximating thunder. And making both men's and ladies' shoes crunch on gravel in a big flat box. Playing around in that back room had been the best thing about that relationship.

"My old grandpa framed it," Myrtle said. "It's my final assignment. Do you remember him? He passed a while ago. I miss him something awful. Should I unwrap it? Do you want me to?"

Again Miss Pearson seemed to try to say something and again no sound came out.

"What was that?" asked Myrtle, leaning forward and holding her hand up to her ear.

Miss Pearson leaned forward too. She licked at her lips. She cleared her throat. Myrtle started to speak into the silence that ensued. She started to say some more about the weather, about one of the assignments Miss Pearson had given them on a rainy day to do with standing in different parts of the room and then writing down what they had heard and felt. Myrtle found she could speak on the subject of that assignment and many others with great detail and might have just gone on and on except that Miss Pearson shook her head. She used a finger to point in the direction of the package and then cleared her throat again and leaned in even closer and said, surprisingly clearly, surprisingly loudly, some six inches away from Myrtle's ear, "F!"

"F?" asked Myrtle.

Miss Pearson's eyes fixed themselves on Myrtle's. They did not blink. She lifted up her hand and wiped her mouth with the back of it. "Did I stutter?" she said.

The laugh that indeed then came roaring out of Myrtle's mouth was a big one, the very biggest, the kind that had once probably too often made her husband cover his ears and dive behind the couch. Indeed, it came so hot and so hard that not only did it make Myrtle think she had turned into an honest-to-God volcano—as Horace had once described it—but both the attendant and the man from the front desk came and jabbed their heads into the room. The identical looks of alarm on their faces made her laugh harder and all she could do, with one hand over her mouth, was point first at the package and then at Miss Pearson. This latter meanwhile must have conveyed some kind of request for extraction because the attendant strode briskly over, took the handles on the back of her chair and looking at Myrtle said, without there being any question at all in it, "Are you all right, Ma'am?"

Myrtle nodded anyway and might even have managed an apology but then Miss Pearson spoke.

"That's mine," she said, indicating the package. And after the attendant had scooped it up, just before she was turned and wheeled away, the old lady patted Myrtle on the leg and said, "I never liked a damn orange, but I do still like the weather." Then she pursed her lips, sucked in a big breath, and blew. One short, sharp puff that Myrtle heard, saw, and felt like she'd been smacked hard but caressed hard, too, all the way home. There she picked up the wallet she had forgotten to bring with her so she could buy the two ice-cold ginger ales, and then checked how the water was coming: real nice. She'd be prosecuting an evening splash for sure. A proposition that Gladys, once she had sucked down better than half her ginger ale at a single swig and they were walking away from her parents' graves, said she would be most happy to get in on.

So they drove back into Bright Creek where, after crossing big Fred Royer out with his funny-looking basset hound, Myrtle loaned her younger friend one of the three new suits she had bought to go with the pool. Myrtle had imagined that as soon as they got in the water they'd paddle around and tell the tale of their hours—discuss Christmas oranges, hurting husbands and grave-side vigils—but the beautiful cool of the rising water kept being all they could think about for a while. When, holding on to the side, both of them kicking their legs slowly, they finally got to it, Myrtle found that all she could come up with was a comment about how lately she kept catching her mouth hanging open. Gladys's long trip through the cornfields to visit with her parents meanwhile seemed to have gotten boiled down to a remark that there at the end, in the flash of the Dodge's headlights when Myrtle had driven up, she'd seen what despite the late hour she felt certain was a cardinal sitting on top of one of the graves.

Cubby

Cubby Rogers was peeling potatoes. He was planning to serve them scalloped with meat loaf, creamed corn, and leftover green beans. Last night's supper had been a hit, and Cubby was hoping to duplicate his success. Madge had seemed especially happy. She'd beamed and asked for seconds of everything. Thirds of the mashed potatoes. Cubby had made a game of it, pretending to be a waiter. He had stood quietly in attendance near the bed after delivering their trays. Bob had said all Cubby needed was a vest and a clean napkin draped over his forearm and the picture would be complete. When Cubby came back in from fetching more iced tea and chicken-fried steak dressed in one of his father's old Sunday suit vests and a white napkin on his arm, Bob and Madge had clapped.

When he had finished peeling, Cubby began cutting the potatoes into slices. He worked slowly because one of the fingers on his right hand was sprained. It wasn't such a bad sprain—hadn't quite needed a splint—but it hurt and it annoyed him that he had to take such care. That he had to take any care at all. Cubby wanted the slices to be thin but not so thin they wouldn't stay tender or would fall to pieces and, God forbid, need to be spooned up. He had a feeling that Madge would appreciate this. That if he got it right she would remark on how his slices were both soft and slim. That they were just the thing. He hoped the potatoes weren't too old. They had looked fine the day before at the Marsh grocery but now, here, on his cutting board, they seemed unwieldy, somehow both soft and hard, and he had to hold on to them more tightly than was comfortable to keep them from slipping away and onto the floor. In addition to his sprained finger, his shoulders ached. And of course his lower back did too. His lower back always ached. He had changed the oil on four cars that morning and had made good progress on a rebuild of Turner Davis's truck. He had done everything as fast as was reasonable so that he could spend the afternoon in the kitchen getting supper ready for his guests. Cubby liked cooking. Years ago, before he took over the garage, he had dreamed of opening a restaurant. Nothing fancy. Something that catered to local tastes. He hadn't kept up and before Madge and Bob arrived had cooked very little since his parents had moved away, but he always enjoyed it when he did.

Cubby carefully buttered the inside of a glass dish and covered the bottom with two layers of the potato slices. He arranged them neatly. For a time he had liked to read cookbooks, and many of them had stressed the importance of arrangement in constructing successful dishes. When he was satisfied, he poured a layer of cheese roux over the rounds. He then sprinkled an extra handful of grated cheddar—a generous handful because he knew how much Bob liked melted cheese—and then set down another double layer of the slices, taking care again with their placement. He poured on more roux, sprinkled more cheddar, and then covered the dish with Saran Wrap for later. He took a few minutes to clean, not just putting the used bowls and measuring cups in the sink but washing them and then setting them on the drying rack so that they would be ready when he needed them. Cubby took great satisfaction in cleaning as he went. He did this in the garage too. He did not understand how people could stand to leave themselves or others a giant mess to deal with later. Madge said she understood this. She had a horror of anyone who wouldn't even put a single stick of butter away when they were done with it, who left the unused parsley lying on the counter, who didn't use a break in the proceedings to wash that skillet or rinse that bowl. When Madge and Bob had first come to stay with Cubby, Madge had often stood in the kitchen with him while he cooked. She had had many interesting observations and suggestions to make. Cubby had enjoyed her presence and missed her a little now that she had mostly joined Bob in bed, where he had been since the day they arrived. "You tell us the minute you want us gone," Madge had said their first night after Cubby had told them to make themselves at home. They had been in the bedroom. Bob had already taken off his shoes and climbed into the bed. He looked very peaceful. Very pleased.

"I won't ever want that," Cubby had said.

He had first seen them at the Countryside Diner on Main. Or rather he had heard them. He had been rotating the bun and nibbling the protruding tenderloin from around the edges of his sandwich, and he had heard a man's voice, Bob's, say, "There's a thousand things I should have done and that I didn't do and that I long ago left lie there just like that." And then a woman's voice, Madge's, say, "Honey, we've got more in common than you know." On his way to the restroom, which Cubby hadn't really had to use, he had gotten a look at them: older but nothing like ancient; posture and clothes from another era; neat thinning hair on both of them, Bob's slicked back and Madge's permed. They had glasses of ice water in front of them. Nothing else. Bob nodded pleasantly and Madge smiled when he passed. They had on coats and it was not the season for coats. Cubby had the special and lemonades sent over to them on his way out. He had spotted them later sitting at the bus stop that hadn't had a bus stop at it in going on twenty years.

Cubby thought about this as, having set the oven to 350, he plunged in his hands to mix up the ground beef, bread, eggs, salt, pepper, and chopped white onion. He liked to do this. Found the texture pleasing. He had of course scrubbed his hands again before starting. It was one thing to work potatoes with some flecks of garage grease still under your fingernails and another to work a loaf this way. When he had kneaded the mixture to his satisfaction and made a handsome mound of it in a blue metal baking dish, Cubby rinsed his hands at the sink and then combined ketchup, mustard, and brown sugar, taking a whisk to it at the end. He poured the tangy result over the top of his loaf. The combined colors were pleasing. They made him think of certain custom paint jobs. Combinations that helped get the emotions going. Not for the first time, Cubby wondered if he ought to put aside his wrenches and break into the customizing business. He slid the meat loaf onto the lower shelf of the oven and the scalloped potatoes onto the top. Thinking of colors and how they set the heart to racing, he pulled the dish of potatoes back out and sprinkled it with paprika. He had learned about this kind of seasoning from one of his mother's friends, Candy Wilson. Candy had taught him more than one trick in the kitchen over the years. The main one was that you shouldn't ever go too crazy with the seasoning. He set the timer for forty-five minutes, pulled an orangeade from the refrigerator, and went outside to sit for a while in the shade.

Originally Cubby had meant to give his father's La-Z-Boy away. As soon as they had left for Cubby's sister's in Wabash, he had dragged it out to the sidewalk and put a "Free!" sign on it, but though at least a couple of people tried it out, no one had taken it and the weeks had gone by. One warm evening after work Cubby had sat down on it himself and had been surprised by how comfortable it was. He had never liked sitting on it in the house, and had always found it to be something of an eyesore, but somehow outside, where it wasn't too big for the room, like the man who had always sat in it, he saw things differently. He took to occupying it for a time every evening after work. He kept it covered with a plastic sheet at night or when rain was forecast, and if every now and again he had to pick off a leopard slug or cricket it had otherwise worked very well. He knew that eventually it would become mildewed or the leg rest would stop working, but that was the way of the whole world anyway and he intended to enjoy it where it was and while he could. For the first few evenings of their stay, Madge had sat with her ankles neatly crossed in one of the lawn chairs next to the La-Z-Boy. She said Bob would have joined them if he had felt up to it. That he had said there was nothing quite so nice as setting and talking in the evening breeze. Horace Allen, Jodi Davis, and Ethel Goodwin, who owned a majority share in the garage and liked to look in on him, had all stopped to visit a while with them. Horace had come more than once. He had seemed unusually talkative to Cubby. Madge had said after he left the second time that it was a good thing she and Bob weren't an item because that way she didn't have to pretend Horace wasn't about the best-looking man she had ever seen.

Bethie Dorner had swung by in her Datsun the evening after Madge had joined Bob in bed. Bethie said she had heard Cubby had been keeping interesting company lately and was hoping to meet his houseguests. If she was disappointed that there weren't any houseguests to be seen, she hadn't said anything and had sat with Cubby for a good long while. They had watched the Keller kids shooting hoops down the street and talked about gas prices and Bethie's daughter and what a godawful job President Reagan was doing down in Washington. Bethie was one of the few people in Bright Creek Cubby could speak honestly with about politics. Most of his fine fellow citizens got all glowy eyed when the subject of the former governor of California came up. Cubby had voted for Democrats since he turned eighteen. He and his parents had fallen out over the Carter administration. His father had called Cubby a turncoat, a traitor to the flag, had said more than once that he ought to be taken out back and shot. He and Cubby's mother had moved out not long afterward. Cubby's sister called him up from time to time and told him about the things they had said about Cubby that day. Apparently, Cubby's father had lately taken to saying he ought to move to Russia. See how his communist butt liked the weather over there in Moscow. Cubby enjoyed sitting outside in his father's old chair and saying nice things about Jimmy Carter. Maybe Carter hadn't been the best president, but there wasn't any doubting his qualities as a person and as a Christian and you knew he wasn't ever going to stop trying to do what was right and good.

After a while of talking, Bethie declared that Cubby was interesting even without any out-of-town houseguests sitting next to him to spice things up. Cubby said a few things about Bob and Madge then. He said they were decent people of varied experience, that they had much to offer, much to impart. Bethie smiled at these generalities, accepting without remark that there wasn't going to be much more, and before long turned the subject to the latest odd cases at the ER, meaning Cubby didn't have to talk around the curious fact that Madge was lying up in the bed next to Bob, a man she had met for the first time the very day Cubby had taken them in, with the covers pulled up to her chin. It wasn't that he minded, or that he thought Bethie would think it was too strange, but he was afraid that if he tried to describe it, words would fail him and he would say it in a way he didn't mean and that would harm it all somehow. *They just want the one meal each day and I bring it to them in bed. Bob hasn't been downstairs since they arrived. They met because Bob put an advertisement in the* Kokomo Tribune *about looking for some short-term adventure, about seeing the countryside. They rendez-vous-ed in Russiaville. Hitched a ride first to Kempton and then on to Bright Creek. They weren't lovers. Both led agreeable lives they could easily return to. Madge had a husband she liked fairly well and grown children who were doing fine. Bob had struggled some lately but until recently had worked for decent money on the line at Delco. They had each proposed a rule for the trip. Bob's had been that they couldn't bring any bags. Madge's had been that they would have to rely for their needs on the kindness of strangers.* They hadn't made any speech about this to Cubby. It had just come out in bits and pieces over the time they had been his guests. It pleased him more than he could say that he had been the stranger offering kindness in their story. Cubby wondered if this aspect of the arrangement was what he would find hardest to put across. It was one thing to say it and another to respond to follow-up questions. But Bethie was easy that way and he didn't even have to mutter things about Christian obligation and lending a hand to those in need.

Bethie Dorner skipped through Cubby's mind more often than just about anyone else in town. He knew that he had thought of her when he sat down to rest from his labors in the kitchen because he had earlier seen her teenage daughter, Della, jump onto the back of a big Suzuki motorcycle captained by Sugar Henry. This had been not long after the start of her shift at the Galaxy Swirl, which stood one lot and some leftover plum orchard away from his garage. She had pumped her fist and Sugar had gunned it on up the street and, as far as Cubby had been able to tell, straight out of town. Cubby knew for a fact that Sugar Henry had neither motorcycle of his own nor license to legally drive it. He also knew that, when, an hour later he had closed the garage and come home to cook, the Galaxy Swirl had been empty. Even Della's puppy-dog lieutenant, Greg Cullen, looked to have abandoned his post. Cubby took a long pull on his orangeade and thought about being fifteen. Doing so made him chuckle. He was still smiling about it when the timer went off and he sloshed down the rest of the drink and went back into the house. The kitchen smelled like the angels had come calling. Which was the way his mother had liked to put it when she had the recipe right. That hadn't happened every time she opened a cookbook. It most definitely had not. Cubby's father had said many a time as they threw open all the windows that he was glad they didn't have a smoke alarm like some people did, that they would have long since gone deaf. Cubby eyeballed the potatoes and then pulled the meat loaf, ladled up some of its juices, and drizzled them over the top. Then he put the blue pan back in the oven and set the timer for fifteen more minutes. He didn't like to yell, so he climbed the stairs and knocked on the bedroom door.

"Supper'll be up in about half an hour."

"Smells just wonderful!" said Madge.

Cubby went back downstairs and put the leftover beans on the stove to heat. He hoped Bob and Madge would have one of their discussions while they ate. They talked about any number of things while they were tucking in. Sometimes their conversations were revealing. The night before, Bob had brought up a young man he said he had once known, a young man who had problems in the head. His family had thought they could cure him a little at least by marrying him off, that fresh curtains and regular marital congress was what would solve his problems. Neither the curtains nor the congress—though the curtains were pretty and the congress had been regular—had led to the desired outcome and the marriage hadn't stuck. "You're talking about yourself, aren't you?" Madge said. "How did you guess that?" asked Bob. Cubby had wondered the same thing but then the conversation switched over to religion and the virtues of the Bethlehem faith. Madge said a number of fine things about the church and what it had to offer society before turning to Bob and, mouth full of mashed potato, saying, "But this thing about Jesus walking on water—can we believe it?"

The phone rang as Cubby was fixing to serve and find out whether Bob and Madge were feeling philosophical. Maybe Madge would tell an interesting story about someone else who was actually herself and he would be the one to guess it. He was curious about Madge. He liked learning things about Bob, but it was Madge who had really captured his imagination. He supposed that was because he had seen more of her. The more you learned about a person the more you wanted to learn. If you liked them. And up to a point. Madge herself had said this. He sensed she had been talking, as they sat out on the sidewalk, about her husband when she said "up to a point," but she hadn't made that explicit and it was only now, thinking about Bob's veiled piece of autobiography, that he could imagine himself having said, "You're talking about your husband, Madge, aren't you?" But when he got to the phone he learned that there had been a wreck and both he and his tow truck were needed and no it sure as shit couldn't wait. Cubby did allow himself to yell upstairs this time. He said he had to go out. That they shouldn't wait on him. That he didn't know how long he would be gone.

Not long as it turned out. Not really. Hurt finger notwithstanding, Cubby knew his business and the old cruiser had come out of the corn easily enough. The corn looked worse off than the cruiser did. Most of the time the chore took had been the standing around after he had the cruiser out on the road and talking about its owner or former owner, depending: retired county sheriff Hank Dunn. Ethel Goodwin had been there. She hadn't been the only one with a tear in her eye. Zorrie Underwood mostly stood there with a hand over her mouth. There was a good deal of hugging. Cubby wasn't necessarily a hugger but he accepted a few. Everybody seemed to have seen Hank at some

point during the day. Jenny Fields said she had spied him sitting
on top of one of his corn bins that very morning like he was the
king of the county. Ethel said, "For a while there he was."

When he had the cruiser towed to the county lot for inspec-
tion and was heading for home, Cubby marveled a little at what
the day had made for him, first seeing Bethie's daughter pumping
her fist and then thinking about visiting with Bethie Dunn
Dorner and then pulling Bethie's father's busted cruiser out of
the field. If that wasn't mystery, he'd like to know what mystery
was. Bob and Madge would likely have a better angle on it, but
in the meantime Cubby thought it was related in kind if not in
quality to the "thing about walking on water." Or to the thing
about Lazarus or to the thing about all those fish and loaves.
Bethie didn't work Thursday nights. Cubby wondered if she
would go back in. Of course she would. Word at the county lot
was it hadn't looked good for Hank. That they had probably
already pronounced. When Cubby got back to Bright Creek, he
swung by Bethie's. Her Datsun wasn't in the driveway. Which
could have meant a number of things but most likely it meant
she had been told. Was Della back from running around with
Sugar Henry? Cubby wondered. Or were they still roaring up
the road, burning up the map, being idiotic and beautiful and
fifteen?

Cubby hoped Bob and Madge had enjoyed the dinner. Who
knew what they had talked about? Maybe when he wasn't there
to listen they didn't say anything. He supposed he should feel
worse about Hank Dunn. He had known him his whole life. Had
even gotten in trouble with him a time or two. Cubby's father
had been the one to administer the actual punishment. His
favored instrument of justice had been a short length of rope.

"You want the fastball, the sinker, or the curve?" his father, who had been a starting varsity pitcher, would ask. Just about everyone had gotten whipped by their daddies back in those days. Still, he didn't think Hank Dunn had ever whipped Bethie. There were surely some things in the world that were just exactly as they seemed.

Take this house of mine, he thought, home again and standing next to the La-Z-Boy, looking down the long walk. When he was still in high school, Cubby had had a summer job working on a demolition crew that knocked things down around the county. The crew boss had come up beside him one early morning on a property near Rossville and said about the little yellow house with its pretty drapes they were about to unleash the wrecking ball on that "you could practically imagine there's someone in there still eating at their oatmeal." Only the place had "the empty feel" and the "empty feel" is what let you know there wasn't anyone home and might not ever be again. When pressed, the crew boss hadn't been able to explain what he meant, but pretty soon Cubby, too, had developed a sense not just about when a broken pane in an upper-floor window wasn't ever going to get fixed because there was no longer anyone to fix it, which was something anyone could figure out, but when a house or an apartment, even one that hadn't been abandoned or condemned, didn't have anyone in it. A girlfriend from that era had dared him to prove it, so after they had driven over to Lebanon, a town neither of them knew so that it would be fair, Cubby had stopped the car outside a well-cared-for house he had straightaway eyeballed as empty, walked right up to the front door, found it unlocked, and opened it. With his girlfriend giggling nervously behind him he had hollered, "Anyone fucking home?" There hadn't been.

Just like there wasn't anyone in his own dark house. Cubby plunked himself down on the La-Z-Boy and tried to decide if he thought Bob and Madge had eaten before they left. He did not. If they had stripped the sheets and put them in the wash. He thought so. If they had taken clean sheets from the hall closet and made the bed. Also yes. He had bought them each a toothbrush, for they were fastidious about keeping their mouths clean. Had they taken those? The tube of Crest? Unsure. But that the house was empty? That Bob and Madge were gone? That his father would vote for Reagan in '84? That Hank Dunn had never laid a finger on Bethie? Definitely. Hank had been the one to come to the store when Cubby was caught stealing Heath bars. He had had two in his right pocket and three in his left. His father had held on to that detail and given him five good whacks with the rope down the backs of his legs when he got home. Hadn't even let him get all the way through the door before he started in. His father had sold insurance policies for the Farm Bureau, had done reasonably well at it. There wasn't any mortgage on the house. There had for years been a late-model car in their driveway. For a while there had been talk of moving down to Indianapolis. Before that could happen his father had been let go. He had found other work, but it had never been the same after that.

Still and all, he had helped Cubby get started with the garage. Before they had fallen out. And they had always gotten their hair cut together. At the barbershop by the square in Frankfort. Where they kept big bags of unshelled peanuts for the customers. You ate as many as you liked and threw the shells on the floor when you were done. Every half hour one of the three barbers would sweep up hair and shells alike. Cubby had gone through a phase of eating the shells along with the peanuts. It had turned into a thing that some of the other customers liked to watch. He could do three at a time. He wasn't that sorry when his father finally told him to cut it out. The shop smelled like peanuts and hair oil and the cigarettes everyone smoked. There was a signed photograph of Gerald Ford on the wall. Cubby missed his father sometimes and wished he would consent, once in a while, to talk with him on the phone. He had always picked "curve ball" and his father had always said "smart boy" before he administered his whacks.

The neon sign over the still-empty Galaxy Swirl had been blinking brightly when Cubby put the truck back in the garage. A small part of the turquoise comet's tail was out, but the purple moon and azure stars were intact. The stars were just regular old blue, but Myrtle Kelly had once called them azure and it had stuck. Cubby wished he could see those stars and that moon and that broke-tail comet from where he sat on the La-Z-Boy. He had for some years thought it was the prettiest thing in Bright Creek. Some people said neon signs were a waste, but they didn't know what they were talking about. When Cubby had driven Bob and Madge back to his house on the first night, Bob had remarked on how handsome the sign was when they drove under it, and Madge had said, "Isn't it though?"

The phones would ring all over town and beyond when Hank was officially declared dead. Cubby's parents had both known Hank well, so Cubby would have to make the phone ring in Wabash. He expected there were people as far away as Chicago who would have to be called. The sign over the Galaxy Swirl would glow and the phones would ring and then the phones would stop ringing and, a little later, the sign would obey the dictates of its autotimer and switch itself off. Sugar and Della were either still speeding away or speeding back home. There weren't that many ways it could be. Or there were. What did Cubby know? He'd had a music teacher in high school named Miss Carrington who had liked to repeat, "A little ignorance goes a long way."

Cubby had just worked himself up to thinking, *yes, of course he walked on water, of course we can believe that*, and wishing he could say it to Madge, wishing she at least hadn't left, when Ethel Goodwin pulled up in her AMC. The summer cold her high emotion had kept at bay earlier was back with a vengeance and she said she wouldn't get out of the car, that she'd been sitting at home praying and waiting to hear and now couldn't stand to be alone.

"Is Della back?" Cubby asked.

"Why, where was she?"

Cubby shrugged. He didn't know where she had been so didn't know how to answer. "Where do you stand on miracles?" he asked instead.

"Where do I stand?"

Cubby nodded.

"You mean on the ones in the Bible?"

"Any miracles. Anything like that."

"Like when the umbrella loan came through for the garage?"

"Something bigger."

"Like the one that's going to happen for Hank tonight? For Hank and Bethie and Della?"

That wasn't quite what Cubby had meant either, but he nodded again.

"What I think about miracles is that we should pray for one. Right now. Right here."

Ethel had to sneeze and blow her nose before she could raise her hands and bow her head, but before long she had gotten going in earnest and Cubby had joined her. In posture at least. For he had never been a champion at prayer. He was nonetheless an admirer of the practice, and had seen the solace its adherents received, especially when they prayed for mercy, grace, or peace. "The peace which passeth all understanding," which his mother had often said she longed for when she was living through something hard, which had been the case as much or even a little more than the average for her during her life in Bright Creek with Cubby's father and probably still was. Thinking about prayer and his mother, with his head bowed and hands clenched as much as his sprained finger would let him there on the La-Z-Boy, Cubby remembered a period during which he and his sister had gotten into crayfish hunting down at the creek. Their father had been working that summer to whip certain bad habits out of Cubby and his mother had begged Cubby to stop and his sister had said that if their father gave the rope a rest she would undertake to cure Cubby. They had gone down to the creek every morning and at some point in the game that went along with the hunt his sister had decided that the crayfish were holy and needed to be prayed to. She said the crayfish were hard to find just like the Good Lord was hard to find and once you had found Him you had to give thanks. It hadn't seemed all that hard to Cubby to find the crayfish, but his sister had been older and controlled the shape of their games, which after all were aimed at keeping their father's rope away from him, and so when they had a crayfish in the little enclosure they had made of rocks and sticks in the shallows they would temple their hands and pray, "Our Craw-daddy, Who art in Heaven, Hallowed be Thy Name, Thy Kingdom come, Thy Crawdaddy Will be done, on Earth as it is in Heaven . . ."

Cubby sat in the La-Z-Boy and let his lips make the shape of this old prayer and whether or not by the time he had finished the phone would have stayed silent or the house would have stopped feeling so empty, as he hoped to Crawdaddy God it would, it seemed to him—"for Thine is the Crawdaddy Kingdom, and the Crawdaddy Power, and the Crawdaddy Glory, Forever and Ever"—a very good one.

Sugar

Sugar? He didn't even like boxing. He thought about it sometimes but not anything like every day. For one thing he wasn't very good at it. An older second cousin who had done all right at the club level and was now assistant manager at a gym over by Kokomo had taught him a few things. Sugar knew how to move his feet some and he knew how to hit the heavy bag. A few times, though, the cousin had had him lace up. "We'll just take it easy. See what you got going on. See what's what." Sugar had him by three inches and twenty pounds and the cousin still beat him silly every time. No one at the gym called Sugar "Sugar." At the gym, he was just Tod. Or Tony the Tank's cousin. Or Tony the Tank's punching bag. Sugar rarely stepped into the ring but the training part, that was all right. He didn't love the roadwork but he was a monster for anything like a pushup. They had pushup contests at the Marsh where he bagged groceries four days a week now that it was summer, and he always won.

Same with pullups. There was a metal bar in the break room. One time he'd done so many that everyone just got bored and walked away. He liked striking poses too. The kind competition bodybuilders got up to. Now there was a sport that made sense to him. You did your training and then you got up on a stage. There wasn't any getting knocked around. Plus poses were symbols, and symbols, if you studied on them long enough, revealed important things to you about the world.

It was striking a pose and then moving his feet and throwing a few decent punches at nothing one day at school when they were all standing in line at the cafeteria that had gotten him his nickname. The teacher who was on lunch duty that day and called him Sugar was also the varsity football coach, so it had stuck. It wasn't a bad nickname. He didn't mind it. After all, some kids in his grade had nicknames like "Fat Ass" or "Pizza Face." Also it was *interesting*. Old Noah Summers's son Max had said so earlier that day, when Sugar had stopped by the Summers's place with his girl Della's grandfather. His girl Della's grandfather had had him listening to stories and driving around and climbing corn bins to scare him or test him or welcome him to the family or something because he and Della had gotten caught getting up to it in the barn that morning. The old man had just driven up to the Marsh and told Sugar to get in. His manager, Beryl Reedy, had said, "Hank Dunn wants you to go somewhere you go," and so off they had gone. Max Summers had not asked Sugar how he had come by his nickname or even if it *was* a nickname: he had just nodded and said he had met a Sugar once up in Chicago, a "singular individual," a someone. They had stood talking in the driveway by Max's orange Volvo station wagon. The Volvo had Illinois plates and a stick shift. Seeing him eyeball it, Max had offered to let Sugar take it for a drive, but he wasn't much better at driving stick than he was at boxing and anyway he had had to get back to work.

"A SINGULAR INDIVIDUAL," Sugar said to a can of Chef Boyardee. He said it with some accent. Or without any accent. The way he thought he'd heard Max Summers talk. Sugar thought it would be nice to know a different way of speaking. At the bank one time with his father, he'd heard old Candy Wilson say she thought somedays everyone sounded like they were talking through spoonsful of seeds and cupsful of dirt. Beryl Reedy had brought in another bagger, since Sugar had been "gone so damn long" and now she had him stocking shelves. Cat food and canned tomatoes and toilet paper for the most part. He'd done it before. Sometimes when an aisle was empty of customers, one or two of the others would try to startle him. That kind of trick worked on most people, but not on Sugar. Sugar was exceptional at not reacting. It was like he was a robot. Even Della's grandfather had said something about it. This made them try even harder. Didn't matter how much Sugar leaned or bent or twisted or tippy-toed to get something where it needed to go on a shelf, he always kept an eye out. Still and all, Butch Harper got him a pretty good one a little later on aisle seven when Sugar was goofing around with some bird-seed bags. He had a ten-pounder of finch food on each shoulder and a five-pounder on his head, and Butch came up behind him and said "Fuck you!" in his ear. Sugar didn't startle exactly but he did blink and Butch saw it and laughed and so he and Butch had to wrestle around. When Beryl came over and called them knuckleheads, Butch went sprinting back in the direction of produce, where, by his own account, he reigned as "king of carrots," "pasha of potatoes," and/or "high lord of lettuce," depending on the day. As the high lord took off, the key to his 1979 dream-blue GS750 Suzuki fell out of his pocket and landed soft on Sugar's work apron, which had gotten torn off in the scuffle. Neither Butch nor Beryl noticed but Sugar sure did. Beryl had already hollered at Sugar for making her put someone else on the clock and then had hollered at him again for saying she was the one who had told him in the first place he had to go with Della's grandfather, and now she hollered at him a third time for fooling around on the job and letting a company apron lie on the floor. When she had hollered herself out, she told him to go home, that she was done dealing with his ugly butt for the day. Sugar said he was sorry and meant it, a little, blew her a saucy kiss because she liked that kind of thing, and then scooped up his apron and went first walking and then running for the lockers.

"SERENDIPITY" WAS A word his mother, Tammy, liked. Sugar spaced out a good deal when she was talking or lecturing, but some things got said frequently enough to come through. He had spaced out some earlier with Della's grandfather. The old man had been a sheriff for a million years and was full of stories and opinions. He kept an old book about a crazy whale in his glovebox instead of a gun. Sugar didn't actually know if sheriffs ever carried guns in their glove boxes but he had seen something like that on TV. Usually when older people like his mother, or Beryl, or Della's grandfather talked to him, he thought of things like being able to dunk a basketball, which he couldn't, or swan diving, which he also couldn't. Even though in the latter connection he had won the ninth-grade gym class diving competition. Pretty much all you had had to do to earn that honor was be willing to fall off the high-dive headfirst. Most had just dropped down feetfirst, holding their noses and saying stupid things. Swan diving was something Sugar associated with Tarzan of the Apes. Tammy told him he thought that because aquatic pursuits had been a specialty of Olympic swim champ Johnny Weissmuller, who had played Tarzan in the early movies. Sugar had pretended to be Tarzan a lot when he was younger. He and his best friend, Greg, had run around the woods pretending they were Tarzan One and Tarzan Two. Each of them had different, though complementary, skills. Broadly speaking, Sugar was good at climbing and jumping and Greg was good at lifting things and sounding like a gorilla. For a long time, Tammy had called them her two Grape Apes, after the cartoon show, and wouldn't serve anything except bananas and Grape-Nuts cereal for breakfast on sleepovers. Tammy was better-than-average funny that way. She made Sugar laugh a lot even when she was lecturing him. He liked to call her Tammy when it was just the two of them at the table or driving along in the car. She grumbled about this but liked it too. You could tell she secretly liked something because her nostrils started to twitch. Sugar supposed that was a tell. Della's grandfather had talked poker for a while. Sugar didn't call her Tammy when she was really mad though. Like she had been that morning. She had used the word *serendipity* to explain how she had learned what he and Della had been getting up to.

Tammy had added the extra two syllables of a participial f-bomb into her use of the serendipity that morning, and it was, in that modified form, what came back to Sugar now as, having extracted the key, he tossed his apron in the locker. It wasn't serendipity that Butch had dropped the key to his sweet wheels where Sugar could scoop them up. It was serendipity that he had done this *and then* Beryl Reedy had cut him loose. Plus it was a beautiful day. That was a lot of serendipity. You couldn't ignore it when that kind of thing happened. Tammy was the one who liked to talk about signs and symbols. How you had to pay attention when you tripped over one. That you would learn things if you did. Like she had practically tripped over Della's tell-tale bike that morning when she was picking trash out of the ditch. Well, it hadn't been exactly like that. But close enough. On his way out, he ducked into the dairy cooler and snatched up a pack of Kraft Singles, which was the coin of the realm. Then set out straight for Bright Creek. No fucking around. That was the message he'd gotten from Della's grandfather. You wanted something, you went after it, you won its heart and brought it home. Old as he was, he had climbed the corn bin and sat down next to Sugar. Had told a story about how he'd met Della's grandmother. About a condition she'd suffered from and a crime she'd helped him solve. Some of the story had been interesting, but Sugar had done his regular spacing out during some of it too, especially the part where Della's grandfather had started acting things out. Sugar had thought about what it would be like to swan dive Tarzan-style off the bin. Had wondered if he could jump far enough from the top to clear the rim. Della's grandfather hadn't noticed. He'd kept telling his story and pointing at things in the distance. Acting like all that hoary old stuff was floating right there in front of them.

Seren-effin'-dipity, Sugar thought. He hadn't had to borrow Butch's Ray-Bans out of his locker because he had his own eyewear. Grocery store eye gear but so what. You couldn't ride without shades. That was a given. *Walk this way. Talk this way.* Etc. A lot of his life was governed by song lyrics. The heavy bike wobbled once or twice when he was tight turning it but not at all when he really opened her up. He hit seventy-five for a stretch of the Kelly road, but kept his cool after that. Took the back lanes. You didn't want to get going too fast on dirt or gravel. Sugar was generally reasonable by nature. His father had more than once called him phlegmatic. It was true that he usually gave things some thought. Greg thought about things way too much. Lately he'd been getting into kung fu. He had a book about it and everything. Before long he'd realize that Sugar wasn't really that tough, that he couldn't really box. Della's grandfather had seen that. Pegged him pretty quick. Sugar felt sure of it. That was probably why he hadn't killed him or at least smacked him around a little.

Sometimes Sugar wrote down what he was thinking about. He liked to find words that rhymed but that wasn't the important thing. He was pretty good at drawing too. He had a notebook filled with poems and sketches that he kept in his sock and underwear drawer. He knew Tammy got it out and looked in it sometimes. Sugar didn't mind as long as she didn't try to talk to him about any of it. Once she had asked him about a drawing of a snake with its head cut off and he had stormed out of the house. Tammy had come out afterward and found him crying. That had made him even angrier. "Wah, wah, wah!" she had said. Pretty soon they were both laughing and she had him in a headlock.

Sugar rode into town past the cemetery. Just about anytime they went by it, Tammy liked to say "Promise you'll visit me" and Sugar liked to say "I'll think about it." He was the apple of his mother's eye. The orange too. That was something else she said. Mainly when he'd done something dumb. That morning she hadn't fooled around with fruits or headlocks and had just shaken

her head and called him a "stupid, stupid boy." Said she wasn't
going to let him turn his life into a train wreck like she had.
Sugar didn't take it personally that the train wreck she was refer-
ring to had been caused by him. He knew she didn't mean it
that way. He knew she meant it in the abstract. The only person
out on Main was Toby Slocum. Sugar tried to beep as he went
past but couldn't find the button in time so he just nodded. Toby
gave him a thumbs-up and waved his Ronald Reagan sign like
a maniac. He was kind of a maniac. Tammy said he had been
born a day late and a dollar short. But Toby Slocum didn't matter.
Sugar was Della-bound. Hell yes he was. *I am a singular individual*, Sugar thought.

Only, funny thing, just as the Galaxy Swirl sundae parlor
where Della worked came spooling into view, Sugar got the idea
that he wanted to arrive from the other direction. That that
would look better. And better was always right. So he braked,
downshifted, slowed almost to a stop, and then, with the big bike
doing its wobble, turned around. He executed this inelegant
maneuver closer to an oncoming El Camino than its driver—she
honked and stuck her middle finger out the window—
appreciated. Not that it much mattered if she was annoyed.
Butch liked to say there probably weren't five cars in the county
that could keep up with him if he didn't want them to and after
about thirty seconds Sugar had left the El Camino and Bright
Creek, too, for that matter far behind. He raised a retaliatory if
almost certainly unseen middle finger into the air and then
turned off the main road with the intention of looping back so
that he could go around the far end of town and pull right up
in front of the Swirl. Struck him, though, that if he kept going
east a while and then just a mile and a half north, in not much
more than five minutes he could be back at the Summers place.

Exchange a few more words with Max. Maybe take that Volvo for a ride and try out his stick-shifting skills. It had crossed his mind earlier to ask Max what he thought of motorcycles and now here he was on one. Probably, though, that would have been stupid, like asking Max what his opinion was on the Flash or Superman, but it seemed to Sugar a different thing entirely to show up on something so fine. Wouldn't stopping by the Summers's place constitute fucking around though? Was he nervous? Was that it? Della wasn't really his girl. They hadn't said anything like that to each other. They were just getting started. Playing games with fake-cheese slices. He wondered what Della would think of his notebook. There were drawings of her in it. He'd tried to do them Heavy Metal style. She wore armor and carried a battle axe. Thinking about her seeing those drawings got his stomach feeling funny. It did a little dance that made him think of the ones Amy Stock sometimes did in the break room. She had a Walkman and about never took it off. Drove Beryl Reedy crazy. Sugar gave up on stopping by the Summers's. He knew what he needed to do.

SIX HOGS HAD once called the played-out shed at the back of their property home. Now there wasn't anything in it except some spools of fencing wire and stacks of cinder block and, at the back by a half-boarded-up window, his stash of cigarettes and reading material. The reading material was some porno magazines he'd had pressed on him by Tony the Tank. Like probably more teenage boys than one might think, Sugar was not a big fan. There was too much to look at. The too much was unsettling. Off-putting even. He'd looked closely at them though. Had on two or three occasions turned their pages slowly with a

Lucky in one hand. Lucky was the brand of cigarette his father had used to smoke. Tammy hadn't smoked since high school. Since she got pregnant with him. His father had quit a few years ago and the subject of cigarettes still made him grumpy. Sugar liked coming to the shed. It was quiet there on the packed dirt. There among the cobwebs he thought about things. If he wanted to, or if there were mosquitoes around and he had forgotten to spray on some Off, he smoked. Greg knew Sugar had a place he went, but Sugar hadn't ever said where it was. He wasn't sure why he didn't want Greg to know. They'd been friends since first grade. Best friends for at least five years. Greg wasn't going to like it later when he showed up at the Swirl on Butch Carter's Suzuki. When he revved that big engine below the neon sign. Greg worked there with Della. He had a crush the size of the Grand Canyon on her. She was the reason Greg had applied for the job. He talked about her a lot. Lately, since she had one morning showed up in Sugar's barn while he was working out, it had been awkward when Greg got going about her shape and looks.

It felt good to catch his breath in the shed, but Sugar wished he had his notebook. He wanted to write down something about the book Della's grandfather had shown him. How could you write something that long about hunting a whale? He couldn't decide if he felt like smoking or not. Sometimes smoking made him feel sick. Tony the Tank said that was probably because he kept letting his Luckies go stale. A lot of the boys at the gym smoked when they were done working out. Last summer he and Greg had smoked down at the creek any number of times. They hadn't done it this summer. There was a lot they hadn't done. Greg had been spending time with little Terry Royer. Sugar liked Terry. You never knew what he was going to come up with. If

Sugar had gone straight to the Swirl, he might have missed
Greg. Della was the opener, so she got there first. Now it would
probably be both of them. And it would all have to come out.
Sugar was tempted to close his eyes. To sleep. He always had
vivid dreams. Just the other night he'd dreamt his father, almost
forty, was a champion long jumper. Over and over his father had
gone flying through the air. Crept into Sugar's mind an image
of Della's grandfather climbing up the corn bin. He wondered
if Della would be climbing corn bins when she was an ancient
old lady. Probably she would.

If he had his notebook, Sugar thought, he would write about
the thistles and Queen Anne's lace growing up around the hog
shed. He would rhyme hog shed with dirt bed and maybe "that
dumb ass's head." He would write about stale cigarettes and the
pint of good whiskey his father kept taped to the bottom of the
seat in the old outhouse. It was an open secret. His father had
quit drinking when he quit smoking. The whiskey was there,
there specifically, so he would have to really want it. The old
outhouse was full of dust. It didn't really smell like much
anymore. Sugar and Greg had untaped the bottle and taken a
swig. They had done it just the once. Tony the Tank had told
him even top-shelf whiskey was an acquired taste. Sugar would
write about the whiskey and he would write about the Illinois
license plate on Max Summers's orange Swedish car. He
wondered what Sweden was like. What it would be like to live
there. Maybe work and get married. Raise a family. Some of
the girls in his Sports Illustrated Swimsuit editions looked
like they were from Sweden. Or somewhere like it.

This thing about Sweden hadn't started with Max Summers's
Volvo. Sugar knew about Sweden because for a while the only
thing he had wanted to have before he went to heaven was a

1970 Husqvarna 400 Cross. Even though it was the bike Steve McQueen made famous, no one else he had talked to besides Greg had even known what Husqvarna was or how to say it, and Greg only knew because Sugar had told him. Sugar had thought that if he had a 400 Cross first thing he would do was gear up and ride his ass straight around the world. When he had pipe dreamed about it, about riding around the world, he had mostly seen himself crossing big deserts with goggles on. He had thought about heat and about sand. Sometimes he would pass men on camels. They would point him on to the next oasis. Where he could drink his fill of cool water and rest his bike. The night before, when for a while during the storm it had really come down, he had been reminded of a ride around the barn lot Tammy had taken him and Greg on. It was back when she was still calling the two of them her Grape Apes, and for a few days they had been making the top of Tammy's Country Squire part of their base. She had kept it parked under a crabapple that had since gone on to its glory and they had used the Squire to get up into the branches and goof around. One afternoon when it started to rain, to really pour, they had stayed out. After a while of it, Tammy had marched out into the deluge. There was a rack on top of the Country Squire, and after she had climbed in and started the engine she hollered out the window for them to lie down on their stomachs and hold on to it. "Hold on, you crazy Grape Apes!" she had yelled and then leaned on the horn, banging on the ceiling of the Country Squire as they went on one hell of a ride. "I'm sorry, Tarzan Two," Sugar practiced as he rolled up in front of the Galaxy Swirl. But it was Della, not Greg, who came busting out of the door.

Bethie

Bethie Dorner woke without waking from ongoing deeper dreams to do with helping save her mother—who never smiled or even thanked her—knowing first thing was she would have to get herself over to Cubby Rogers's filling station and pick up some Tab. This was a matter of some urgency. Not to put too fine a point on the pencil but since she had finally turned her back on Boone's Farm, Tab had become the indispensable ingredient of Bethie's earthly existence. It had become her life's indisputable sine qua non. No Tab cola no Bethie Dunn Dorner was how she had sung it to herself on many a bleary morn. She had thought the afternoon before when she had gone off to work with three cans and a cheese sandwich in her cooler and had stupidly hollered back behind her that, yes, her daughter, Della, could have that last one in the fridge, that there was a fresh six-pack in the garage. Later, though, she had remembered, mid-second-appendix surgery of what had been an unusually busy night, that she had miscounted the last time she was at the Marsh. Cruel error. Because it meant she would have to step out into the wicked summer sunlight without first having enjoyed even a drop. She had almost told Della to get her little last-soda-slurping butt over to the filling station and remedy the situation, but at some point during the dream Della had preempted by announcing she was leaving home to get a scuba diving certificate. That girl never quit. Now she must be off at work. She was a lawyer in Indianapolis. Or a dentist in Muncie. Had her own practice. Practically ruled the town. Bethie could tell she had just missed her. The powdery sweet scent of Love's Baby Soft was everywhere. It was like the bottle had broken and taken over the whole house.

The AC/DC T-shirt Bethie had done her dead mama dreaming in was still on her and would do just fine for the errand but her lower half not so much. Given that she'd recently sworn off shorts, it was down to either of the two relatively clean things she had in the house, sweats or scrubs. Only the first-choice sweats tore completely in half when she was pulling them on, so scrubs it was. She hated wearing anything to do with work when she wasn't on the job. It made her feel like she had to wash her hands every five minutes. She'd do laundry first thing she had some beverage in her. For a second she could see through the walls of the house and what she spotted were mostly Della's clothes, strewn along the hallway like storm wreckage. Luckily, Bethie's washing machine was the size of a basketball gym. Once she'd gotten her Tab situation under control, she'd do a great big load.

Bethie had the keys to her Datsun out and ready, but lying across the front of its hood was Della's ten-speed. Nifty thing. Gift from Bethie's father, Daddy Hank. Della could get down the road well enough, but Bethie was a bona fide whiz on two wheels. Daddy Hank had started her out early on three and had always made sure as she shifted over to two that she had the ride she needed to get the job done. Bethie had been known in the old days as the first girl in town who could not just pop but hold a wheelie. Helped that Daddy Hank had gotten her a Schwinn Stingray. She'd given lessons on the skill, had organized competitions, had even once ridden all the way around the block on her back wheel. Well, halfway around the block. She'd touched down her front tire a short half-second in a blind spot behind Henderson's big sycamore, and the only one who'd seen had been little Toby Slocum. He had stood there watching her, and after her front tire had touched down and before she had gotten it back up she'd put a finger to her lips and Toby had nodded. He must have cut across some yards because he ended up at the finish line at about the same time she did, and though she worried he might squeal, all he did was cheer with the rest of them. When two boys tried after her and didn't even make it to the first turn, let alone to the blind spot by Henderson's, she'd been the hero of the week.

Bethie mounted up and was at the station in two minutes. Ethel Goodwin stood sniffling next to a magenta Camaro at one of the pumps. Mostly it was full serve but everyone knew Ethel was Cubby Rogers's principal investor and so had certain privileges.

"Cubby's out back in the shop, working on Turner Davis's airplane," Ethel said. She sounded terrible, like there was something evil living in her throat. Bethie said she didn't care about what Cubby was working on, she was hunting Tab. Ethel shook her head, sniffed loudly, and offered up a mournful smile. When Bethie got inside she learned why. The place where the Tab always sat was empty. Cubby came in wiping his greasy hands with a rag. He said Bethie would have to go into Frankfort, that there wasn't even the ghost of a can in Bright Creek. Bethie said it would take a week to get to Frankfort on a bicycle. Cubby shrugged his shoulders and offered her a Dr Pepper. Bethie hated Dr Pepper, but she took a drink anyway. It was warm and tasted like Cap'n Crunch. Cap'n Crunch cereal was Della's favorite. Sometimes Bethie ate it too. One time when they were out of milk she poured Tab over it. Della hadn't let her live that one down. When she turned to tell Cubby about this, she saw he was heading out the door.

Bethie followed and handed him back the Dr Pepper. He took a long drink, crushed the can, and dropped it onto the ground. She told him she thought he was cute. That she didn't care if he'd been sitting on the La-Z-Boy too much and had put on a few pounds. They kissed for a while. Bethie found it pleasant and wondered why she hadn't ever agreed to go out on a date with him. He really wasn't bad looking. He was at least as good looking as Daddy Hank had once been and *he'd* gone out with all the old ladies in the county. She told Cubby she thought he could be a surgeon if he wanted to. He said he was actually a surgeon and then showed her a car he had been working on in his spare time. It looked like something from that movie with John Travolta and Olivia Newton John. It bothered her there in her dream that she couldn't remember the title of it. Cubby couldn't either. She asked how it was coming with Turner Davis's airplane. "His airplane?" Cubby said. They kissed some more and Cubby leaned in close to her ear and whispered that he was a surgeon of love and Bethie said, "What I'm talking about."

Her bike was exactly where she had left it in front of the station. Ethel Goodwin was still there pumping gas, though, an hour, maybe more, had gone by. She seemed much improved. They talked about summer colds. Here one minute and gone the next. Just like people! Just like life! Ethel winked at Bethie and gave her the thumbs up. Bethie started to protest, said she and Cubby had only kissed, but Ethel shook her head and pointed down at the bicycle. It wasn't Della's ten-speed anymore. It was Bethie's old Stingray. All brand-new again. It was the first day she had ever owned it and she was the proudest girl in Bright Creek. "I'll be able to get to Frankfort in no time on this," Bethie said. But Ethel wasn't there anymore. In her place stood Bethie's mother. She looked just like Zorrie Underwood, who lived out by Hillisburg, but Bethie knew it was her mother. The way you know things in dreams. Bethie tried to hug her, but she pulled away. She looked stern, upset. She smelled like Della's Love's Baby Soft but curdled. Like Love's Baby Soft made of old milk.

"You haven't had your Tab yet today, little girl," her mother said.

Bethie began weeping uncontrollably. She tried to hug her mother again and this time, to her relief, her mother let her. She even lifted one of her arms and patted Bethie's back.

"There, there," her mother said. "Is that what you wanted?"

"Yes, ma'am," said Bethie.

Her mother seemed to like being called ma'am. Her other arm rose up and the hug now came from both sides.

"I died in my late twenties not too damn long after giving birth to you," she said.

"Yes, ma'am," Bethie said again.

"You were the end of me."

"I know I was."

"I know I was, *ma'am*."

"I know I was, ma'am."

"It broke your Daddy's heart."

"Yes, ma'am."

Her mother suddenly stepped back and shoved Bethie away from her, so hard she fell against her Stingray and knocked it over and scraped her elbow on the asphalt.

"But it didn't break it near enough!" her mother hissed.

"You're just hateful," Bethie said, standing up and rubbing at her arm. "You're just," she repeated, picking up her Stingray and swinging a leg over it, "hateful."

"I was nice once upon a time," her mother said thoughtfully.

"You mean before you died?"

"I don't remember when."

"I've got to go, Mama."

"You've got to get your Tab."

"Yes, ma'am."

Her mother now looked like the picture Bethie had had in her bedroom growing up. She had been pretty. Like someone in a song. The Stingray's tires were on the low side but she thought they would do.

"What is AC/DC?" Bethie's mother asked.

"It's just a band, Mama," she said.

"Are they any good?"

Bethie shrugged. "It's Della's T-shirt. I think she stole it from Greg Cullen. Or maybe Sugar Henry."

Bethie's mother sighed. "I don't know who those people are. My name was Darla Dunn when I was living. It was Darla Henderson before that. I was alive once. I was living. I lived on this earth."

Bethie didn't know what to say, so didn't say anything. When she started to pedal, Cubby came out of the shop with his greasy rag and waved her off.

TO BETHIE'S DISMAY, it quickly became evident that the tires were going to be a problem. She wished she had had Cubby put some air in them, even considered turning back, but when she looked over her shoulder it wasn't just the gas station but the entire town around it that was gone. *That's because I'm dreaming*, she said to herself. Sleeping and dreaming were something of a specialty with Bethie. Had been since early on. Daddy Hank had sometimes had to holler in her ear to get her ready for school. "Sleep deep / Dream hard . . ." had been the motto of her senior yearbook page. At work they joked that she slept—in the middle of a shift on one of the cots in the big closet outside Operating Room One—like she had been sucking on the isoflurane, like she wouldn't even feel it if they started prepping her. It wasn't that she couldn't get up when she wanted to, say when nature called (Della had caught her staggering back from the bathroom that very morning and made her go outside to see her off on a run) or it was time to get back to work (everyone knew not to hand her anything sharp for the first five or ten minutes though). But given her druthers, well, Bethie went all in when it was getting-horizontal-time. Meaning that, given how much of her life she spent doing it, there wasn't anything too out of the ordinary about knowing where and in what state she was. Not that it ever helped. She couldn't get this dream she knew was happening to do anything for her. Certainly, she couldn't get it to fill her tires up with air. In fact, before she knew it the tires were gone entirely and she was rolling through Bright Creek on the rims. Pretty soon, she could feel them starting to warp and bend. There was an ugly scraping, crunching sound. For fifty yards or so, she yarred left and right as much as she moved forward.

She was almost glad, then, that as she was passing the library she heard someone say "Pssst!" Thinking it was someone who could help her with her tires, she made her way over to the curb. Whoever had hailed her was concealed behind one of the overgrown evergreens that grew next to the library steps.

"Come back here," a voice said.

"But I've got my bike. I can't leave it. Someone'll steal it."

"No, they won't."

"They might."

"Might doesn't mean much."

She thought she recognized the voice but couldn't be sure. There was a small space between the evergreen and the steps. Not wanting to take any chances she brought the Stingray with her. Fortunately, she was able to fold it up and tuck it under her arm.

"I just need some air," she said.

"That doesn't matter anymore," the voice said.

"But I can do wheelies!"

"Anyone can do a wheelie."

"That's just not true."

"Ask *them* if it's true or not."

"Who?"

"Whom. Go back out to the sidewalk and see."

"But I don't want to."

"What you want doesn't matter. It's all right. They're all on the street. Go take a look."

Curious, Bethie turned around. She had gone farther from the sidewalk than she had realized. The evergreen was as big as a woods. Pretty soon she had to crawl. She tucked the Stingray into the waistband of her sweats so it wouldn't fall. It hadn't had a horn before but now it did, and the horn turned out to be a mouth and it said encouraging things to keep her going. She explained to it that she really just wanted a nice cold drink of Tab and then to wake up.

"You think when you wake up there'll be Tab?" asked the Stingray.

"I know there will be. It's just in this damn dream I don't have any."

"Tab isn't good for you."

Bethie wondered if the Stingray had been the one speaking to her all along. It might have thrown its voice to make her think it was behind the bushes. You never knew what could happen when your eyes were closed.

"Just a little farther," it said.

"I'm so confused," Bethie said.

Usually when her dreams went sideways she didn't get where she had been hoping to go, but after slithering forward the last stretch on her belly, she found herself back out on the sidewalk.

Practically the whole town was there. And they were all on chopper bikes. In every color of the rainbow. They were so bright she could hardly stand it. They were riding back and forth, around and around, many of them pulling wheelies. Impressive ones. Best of all at it was Daddy Hank's old flame Irma Ray. Bethie supposed that if you had what it took to get people, including Daddy Hank, to help you fake your own death so you could go ghosting off with middle finger raised to the other side of the world you might have some skill at making a bicycle do tricks. Still, all the wheelie-ing going on was chafing her.

"I'm the one knows how to do the damn wheelies!" she yelled.

"Not anymore you don't," the Stingray said. Its voice had changed. When she looked, she saw it had become its namesake and was floating before her. Everything was now under water. They were at the bottom of the sea.

"You have to swim now, Bethie," the Stingray said.

"We'll follow you," Wendell Bacon called.

"Lead the way," hollered Candy Wilson.

"Come on, Mama!" Della cheered.

Bethie started to swim. She realized they would only be able to hold their breath for so long, that she would need to lead them to the surface. But where was the surface of a dream? At first, she swam straight down Main Street with the Stingray in front of her and everyone else right behind. When she got to the edge of town and saw huge sharks and schools of tuna and whales cruising out between the corn bins and out over the fields, she knew her only option was to swim up as fast as she could. Somehow the few dozen citizens behind her had turned into thousands. Even as she finally breached the surface and took a deep gulp of air, she could see that some hadn't even left the ground and the only way to help them now was to keep moving, up through the air and then out into space.

She found that a combination of swimming and flying worked best. The higher she went the harder it was to keep going.

"Isn't that just the shits?" the Stingray asked her. It really was a marvelous creature. So powerful and handsome and deadly.

"You wouldn't ever sting *me* would you?" she said.

"Depends," the Stingray said.

"You're as mean as my mother."

"Maybe you're the one who's mean."

While they talked, everything around them grew black. Stars fizzed in the distance. The moon looked huge.

"Are they all safe now? Did we make it?" Bethie asked.

The Stingray told her to look behind her and see for herself.

"But if I look behind me everything will be gone."

"Have a little faith."

"Are you Jesus?"

"No, I'm your bicycle."

"But you got stolen years ago."

"That's true. Doesn't make me Jesus."

"Are we in space?"

"Where do you think we are?"

"I just wanted some Tab."

"You sure that's all you wanted."

"Yes."

"Then you'll have to go back."

Bethie turned. The earth was a ball of blue and white against the starlit black.

"Where is everyone?"

"They're still down there."

"Where?"

"You see that part where it's green?"

"I can't see it."

"Well, that's where they are."

"Did they drown?"

"No."

"They're all right?"

"Honey, they're just fine."

"Every one of them?"

"Most of them are fine."

"Who isn't?"

"Go back and see."

"I think you are Jesus. Or God. You're the Good Lord, aren't you? I think that's who you are."

The Stingray shrugged and swam off. Or was it more accurate to call it flying? She wasn't sure. Somewhere a phone was ringing. Even all the way out there in space. Bethie knew she ought to answer it. Really, she should. Someone told her it was time to wake up—"Wake up now, my darling . . ."—but Bethie, dreaming, dreamed on.

ACKNOWLEDGMENTS

Though *Float Up, Sing Down*, like *Indiana, Indiana* and *Zorrie* before it, is set in Clinton County, Indiana, where my family has deep roots, the town of Bright Creek and its principal inhabitants are fictional.

Sincere thanks to Hoosiers Stephen Hunt and Carolyn Anderson for invaluable fact-checking, as well as for their generosity in sharing memories from the rural Indiana of their youth. Eva Sikelianos Hunt and Lorna Hunt were with me on many a research trip back to the family farm where I spent my teens. A special shout to Gabrielle Rilleau for inspiring an important scene. I couldn't have written this book without the unwavering belief and unending encouragement, all down these last decades, of Eleni Sikelianos.

Huge thanks also to Callie Garnett, Jillian Ramirez, Akshaya Iyer, and Rosie Mahorter at Bloomsbury, Jon Riley at Riverrun, and to Anna Stein and Claire Nozières at CAA and Lucy Luck at C&W.

I am grateful to MacDowell for the gift of time and space to complete these tales.

A NOTE ON THE AUTHOR

LAIRD HUNT is the author of eight novels, two collections of stories, and two book-length translations from the French. His most recent novel, *Zorrie*, was a finalist for the National Book Award. Hunt has been a finalist for the PEN/Faulkner Award for Fiction and won the Anisfield-Wolf Award for Fiction, the Grand Prix de Littérature Américaine, and Italy's Bridge Award. His reviews and essays have been published in the *New York Times*, *Washington Post*, *Los Angeles Times*, and many others. He teaches in the Department of Literary Arts at Brown University and lives in Providence.